NOT JU

Sally Christie kept a number of animals when
she was a child, including a goat, the eponymous
heroine of her first novel, *Not Just Jemima*,
which was shortlisted for the 1991 Writers'
Guild Children's Book Award. She was once
tempted to train as a vet and later tried to get
a job on a city farm, but ended up as a children's
book editor. She now lives in a gardenless first-
floor flat in London where a goat would
definitely not be allowed. She's considering
taking on Chinese quail instead!

Sally Christie has written one other book for
younger readers, *Weedy Me*.

"The author obviously knows and loves goats…
I liked this gentle book."
Gene Kemp
The Times Educational Supplement

"Sally Christie has a sharp eye for the detail of
group relationships and a sharp ear for the
special, elliptical exchanges in which they
communicate."
The Children's Book Foundation's 100 Best Books

Also by the same author

Weedy Me

SALLY CHRISTIE

Not Just Jemima

~~Effort~~

Effort prize

Janice Dey

34, Cloyfin Park

WALKER BOOKS
LONDON

First published 1990 by Julia MacRae Books
This edition published 1992 by Walker Books Ltd
87 Vauxhall Walk, London SE11 5HJ

Reprinted 1992

© 1990 Sally Christie
Cover illustration © 1990 Wendy Hoile

Printed and bound in Great Britain by
Cox & Wyman Ltd, Reading, Berkshire

British Library Cataloguing in Publication Data
A catalogue record for this book
is available from the British Library.

ISBN 0-7445-2301-X

Contents

DIARY LESSON

Jemima. When Tamsin had dotted the 'i' and put in the full stop, she couldn't think of anything more worth writing about. But there were still eleven minutes to go before the end of the lesson, and she mustn't seem to be at a loss or Mr Lively might make her start something else.

Thoughtfully, with her fingertips, she stroked the words she had just written; but the full stop and the dot on that last 'i' hadn't properly dried. Little bright beads of wet ink, they smudged under her touch. Now, trailing their own fade-out speed marks, the dots looked as though they had just that moment rushed into their places from somewhere on the right of the page.

Tamsin sighed. Why did she always have to go and stroke the page after she'd finished writing on it? Last year, when she was still at primary school, it hadn't mattered because everyone wrote in pencil. But now, at Swinston Secondary, they all had to write in pen – and Gregory Salter had started a craze for proper cartridge pens.

Suddenly Tamsin knew that she hated Swinston. She hated everything about it. Teachers, lessons, children; Gregory Salter and his stupid pen. Even children who had been her friends at primary school seemed to have changed since coming here. . .

Five minutes to go, now, before the end of the lesson. Tamsin read over her last two sentences. 'I do not know what she will be like. Her name is Jemima.' Probably, those two sentences were not allowed, because they broke Mr Lively's Friday afternoon rules. At the beginning of term, he had made Friday's English lesson into a 'diary lesson', when everybody had to write down what they'd done during the week.

"You see," he had said, "there are two kinds of diary: engagement diaries and journals. You use an engagement diary for planning ahead, but in a journal, you describe things you've already done. Each one of you is going to build up that kind of diary this term. *The Summer Term of My First Year at Swinston*, you can call it. If you write accurately about what you've been doing and how you've been feeling, you'll find it a fascinating account to look back on in years to come."

Yes, the more Tamsin thought about it, the more certain she was that her last two sentences *were* breaking the rules – by venturing into the future tense instead of sticking to things that had already happened. But it wasn't a very distant future she was thinking about: tomorrow she would go next door to baby-sit for Mrs Plummer, and then she would find out what Jemima was like. Besides, she didn't want to write down the things that had happened to her during the week. They were all dull and disappointing, and if she was going to look back on this diary in years to come, she didn't want her older self to be reminded of how she'd wasted her spare time doing things she could only pretend to enjoy.

"OK, it's just about quarter to four." Mr Lively's voice sounded relieved and weary – less Welsh than usual. "You can stop writing now, 1L, and put your diaries away."

There was a general rustling of paper and a zipping-up of pencil cases. People began talking to their neighbours again, after the forty minutes' silent concentration.

"No, Paul." Mr Lively's voice rose above the chatter. "Don't put your diary in your locker. In your bag, lad, in your bag. You've got homework to do, remember?"

"But sir, diary homework's not fair." Paul Peck, like Gregory Salter, had come from Swinston Village Primary – not the primary school that Tamsin had been to. Although he wasn't as tall or as good at sport as Gregory (and he'd never bothered to get himself a cartridge pen), he was better than anyone else at answering teachers back without getting put into detention. Of course, with some teachers you couldn't answer back at all. But you could, if you were clever, with Mr Lively. Good old Livers was all right, really.

"Paul, diary homework is perfectly fair. Now shut up and put that book in your bag."

"But sir, if we have to write about the weekend, then we've got to wait till Sunday night, and I have to go to church at six and then Auntie comes round afterwards and I won't have time to do any homework then." Wide-eyed, breathless mock-innocence.

"Paul, shut up, shut up, shut up! You can write your diary *before* six on Sunday – OK?"

"But sir, then I won't be able to write about Auntie – and she's a real laugh, my auntie is. The best things always happen when Auntie comes round. After church. On Sunday night."

Somebody at the back of the class began thumping their desk as a sign of applause, and somebody else gave a low cheer.

"Paul, you are a thoroughly irritating little idiot. Now, tie a knot in it –" the whole class whooped and whistled "– and I want that diary handed in on Monday with the weekend written up, auntie or no auntie. See?"

"But sir . . ."

"Have a good weekend, everyone. See you all on Monday. Off you go."

Sitting next to Tamsin, Jessie Lawson was still frantically scribbling. Jessie was Tamsin's best friend from primary school. In each diary lesson of the first half of that term, she'd had so much to write that she'd had to use up every moment of lesson time, or she'd have ended up finishing off in her own time, as extra homework. This Friday – the first after half term – was the same as ever before.

Now Jessie at last flipped shut her exercise book and stuffed her things into her bag. She and Tamsin left the classroom together.

"How come you had so much to write, Jess?" Tamsin asked.

"You could have written just as much as me," said Jessie. "You know – all about how everyone goes round to Greg's after school, and what good fun we have."

"Yes, but we've gone round his every day this week, and each time we've done exactly the same things."

"So? So you write everything down four times over. You have to, to be accurate, like old Livers said."

Jessie suddenly broke into a run, to catch up with Gregory. "Come on, Tats," she shouted behind her to Tamsin. "Let's all bundle round Greg's again now."

Gregory lived in Swinston itself, not far from the school. Because Tamsin and Jessie cycled to school, they didn't have to worry about catching buses at the end of the day. They could just about fit in an hour at Greg's before setting off back for their own village, Great Whenock, to be home in time for their teas.

The little group that had gathered around Gregory paused on its way to the school gates, while Jessie and Tamsin collected their bikes from the bike sheds. When they all reached the gates, Paul Peck split off from the rest and walked down the street by himself. He'd gone off like that, after school, ever since half term: a whole week of not going round to Greg's.

"What's the matter, Pecky?" shouted Greg. "Got to go and make tea for Auntie?"

"Ha ha, very funny, Greg," Paul shouted back. "Nope, Auntie makes her own tea, thanks. I've got other things to do. Other things *apart* from going round yours every day – wildly exciting though that may be."

Greg laughed, but he didn't look as if he really found it funny. Jessie said, "I bet it *is* his auntie, and he's too embarrassed to say so."

"Yeh," said Greg, "I bet that's it. Pecky's boring outside school, anyway. We're better off without him."

Tamsin watched Paul walking away from them, as you might watch somebody tumbling into a tiger trap you'd been about to step on yourself. She too had been considering going straight home today, without going to Greg's first, but now she changed her mind. "Come on, you lot," she said suddenly and rather loudly. "It's already nearly four. There won't be time for anything if we hang about here all day."

10

2

CHICKEN

The good thing about going round to Gregory Salter's was that Gregory Salter had a place all of his own. He had a bedroom, of course, but he also had a room quite separate from the house. Greg's parents had converted the loft above the garage into a sort of den, with odd scraps of carpet and old cushions and a little square window at one end. They'd done it, originally, for Greg's older brother, Stephen. Then Stephen had got a motorbike, and a leather-trousered girlfriend to go with it, and Greg had been allowed to take over the loft. For his last birthday, his parents had wired it up to the mains electricity supply. So now there was a light bulb there, although the switch was down below, in the garage, by the foot of the ladder that you had to climb up to reach the trapdoor.

'Greg's loft is brilliant,' Jessie had written (four times over) in her diary that afternoon. She'd written about playing darts there every day, with the dartboard hung so near to the floor, because of the low, sloping ceiling, that you had to throw from a sitting position. She'd written about playing cards there every day, lounging round in a circle on the lumpy cushions. She'd written about listening – every day – to the radio, with the volume turned up high, and about eating fish and chips every day from the fish and chip shop round the corner. To make each day sound different in the diary, Jessie had here and there swapped 'but' for 'however', and 'then' for 'next'. She'd also pointed out the different take-aways that she'd eaten: on Monday it had been cod and chips (large portion); on Tuesday, fish cake and a large chips; on Wednesday, a large portion of chips on its own; on Thursday, a small chips. (Parents raged that their children hardly ever seemed hungry when it came to tea time, but the explanation remained a mystery.)

And now it was Friday. If Jessie had had a little more time at the end of the diary lesson, and just a very little more imagination, she could have written up Friday evening as well, in advance. She could even have predicted what take-away she'd be buying – or wouldn't be buying – since she hadn't got enough money left for any kind of take-away at all. But it was lucky that she hadn't written about after school on Friday, not only because the future was out of bounds in their journals, but also because this Friday, in Greg's loft, something a bit different happened.

There were five of them in the loft today: Greg, Jessie, Tamsin, a boy called John Crescent and a girl called Karen Halliday. They were playing twenty-one, betting with the small change that hadn't been enough to buy them portions of chips. Friday was always like that. On Saturday there would be pocket money and paper-round wages, but on Friday they were skint.

Today, Tamsin deliberately played badly and allowed herself to go broke. Going broke had seemed the safest way out. She'd considered announcing openly that she didn't feel like playing any more, but then she'd remembered Paul's saying he didn't feel like coming along with the rest. She remembered what Greg and Jessie had said about him, and she decided to keep quiet about being bored with twenty-one.

So Tamsin went broke – and made a big fuss about how it wasn't fair, and she couldn't believe it, and it was enough to make you think that people must be cheating. Jessie said, "Bad luck, Tats," quite sympathetically, and even Greg said, "Yeh, bad luck" – so that was OK. Tamsin moved away to look out of the window.

Through the glass, she could see Greg's garden, with another garden backing on to it – then a strip of allotments, then the railway line – and beyond that, open fields. She fixed her gaze on the clumpy black outline of a tree that poked up from a hedgerow dividing two large fields. She tried to focus all her thinking on that tree and, by shutting

12

everything else out, she could imagine herself there. She imagined herself sitting at the foot of the tree, quiet and alone.

It was a trick she sometimes used in lessons at school. She would fix her eyes on an 'o' somewhere on the page of the textbook in front of her and then, in her imagination, she would climb inside and find herself back in the dear old classroom at Whenock Primary School. In the world inside that 'o', nobody had to write in pen, nobody was given homework, and she could always be sure that Jessie liked her better than anyone else in the class.

Tamsin stared on at the tree. The bark would perhaps be rough against her back, and there might be a nettle to sting her ankle, but she would be quiet and alone. She would be far away from the blare of the radio and far away from Jessie being so matey with Greg.

Then she heard Jessie shouting to her, above the radio noise: "Hey, Tats, come back over here! John's got to go now, so we're stopping, but we'll be all right for darts doubles. You and Karen, me and Greg."

"Coming," Tamsin answered. She didn't want to leave her tree, but she didn't dare to stay. What would it be like if Jess and Greg and the others ever began thinking she was some kind of weirdo – if she ever stayed away by herself and they said, 'We're better off without her'? That would be a different sort of alone from the sort she chose for herself, under the distant tree.

Tamsin withdrew her eyes from the tree. Reluctantly, she brought her gaze sweeping back across the fields and over the railway line. A train came and went. She brought her gaze in closer, to the allotments. There was a man in one of them, and a small flock of white hens. The man was facing away from Tamsin so that, until he flung it from him, she didn't realize that he'd been holding one of the hens.

The hen fell to the ground when it was thrown, without squawking or flapping its wings. It landed on its back, wings lying limply open and neck twisted round in an impossible position. Only its legs moved. Again and again they jabbed upwards into the air, senselessly and uselessly going through the motions of escape. If only the hen had been the right way up, thought Tamsin, those legs would have been carrying it away. Away from the allotment and the man and the cruel, neck-wringing hands.

She felt sick with despair. It was terrible: a thing that behaved as if it had a chance, when actually it was done for – dead already. She wished and wished that it would lie still, and then there wouldn't be so much to feel sorry about.

"Tam-sin!" It was Jessie's voice calling, in mimicry of somebody calling to somebody else over a vast distance. "Are you com-ing?"

"Yeh, come on," said Greg. "In a trance, are you? Don't you want to play in our game?"

Tamsin heard, and was suddenly scared, and panicked. "Yes," she said loudly. "Yeh. Course. Only I was looking at something out of the window. Something really – funny."

She hadn't wanted to say that at all. But it had been the only thing to do, hadn't it? She'd wanted to screw her fists into her eyes and cry, but she knew that, instead, she must laugh with the others at the hen. She had to do that. It was vital.

They were already getting up and coming over to see. They crowded round the window, and Tamsin pointed towards the poultry-keeper's allotment and said, "There – look."

"Wow!" said Greg. "I don't believe this! It's fab! What a crack-up!" He grinned and stared and chuckled. Jessie shrieked and snorted and had to clasp her arms about her chest because she was laughing so much that it hurt. Tamsin laughed, too.

Karen was clutching Greg's arm and screaming "Ugh" and "I'm gonna be *sick*" over and over again, in a fit of put-on hysterics. Karen Halliday was like that: always on about how she reckoned she'd been Greg's girlfriend at primary school, and always trying to do things to prove it, although Greg mostly ignored her.

Now the hen's legs were beginning to slow down. Round and round they went, but less frantically than before.

"My dad's wrung lots of chickens' necks," said John Crescent, putting on his coat. "That's nothing. I tell you, my dad's seen their legs go much faster than that." Mr Crescent worked on the farm next to Swinston Village Primary. John had been an important person in Greg's class there last year, because whenever a football had gone over the playground fence, he'd had to be the one to climb over into the cornfield to get it back.

"Once, on the farm, Dad even saw a dead chicken fly up into the air," said John.

"Oh yeh?" said Tamsin. "I bet your dad's never seen a chicken that looks like it's riding on an upside-down bike. That's what this one thinks it's doing: pedalling. That's what Paul would look like if you held him on his back and told him to cycle round to Auntie's."

Jessie laughed louder than ever at that. "I can just see it," she gasped. "Pecky the Pedaller! Pedalling Paul Peck!"

The most miserable thing in the world, Tamsin thought then, was to laugh at something with a bunch of other people and to know that you were only pretending to laugh, while everyone else really did think it was funny. Tamsin felt lonely, which was odd because she'd started the joke in the first place to keep in with the others. It was all so confusing – so difficult always to make the right decision.

"I'd better go now," she said, looking at Jessie. "Mum and Dad were cross last time I got back after five thirty. It's all right for you, staying till the last minute – your bike's faster than mine."

Tamsin hadn't meant to suggest that Jessie *should* stay longer, and that she herself should go on ahead. But Jessie said straight away, "OK. See you. See you tomorrow night. I'll come round for you and we'll all go into town or something."

"No," said Tamsin. "Can't come out tomorrow." And just as Jessie was about to argue, she said, "I'm going baby-sitting, remember?"

All the way back from Swinston to Whenock, Tamsin thought about baby-sitting. She thought about how it was letting her out of an evening with Jessie and Greg tomorrow. What a piece of luck it had been, Mrs Plummer's asking her to do it! And how lucky that her parents had agreed to let her, even though she was still really too young. Jess and the others thought baby-sitting was OK because it was an easy way of earning money, and Tamsin felt rather important because nobody else she knew at school had ever done it before. Yes, baby-sitting was the perfect let-out: something that no one would expect her to turn down.

And then, of course, there was Jemima. Tamsin hadn't mentioned her to anyone – she'd just told them that she was doing this because she wanted the money. But more than the money, she wanted to see Jemima. She'd thought so much about her, ever since the Plummers had moved in next door, three or four weeks ago. And tomorrow night she would see her – she'd already heard her – perhaps even touch her. Thinking about Jemima was better than thinking about being back at primary school or imagining yourself sitting under a far-away tree. Because Jemima was real.

BABY-SITTING

"Now remember," said Tamsin's father, "if you want us, just phone, and we'll be round straight away."

"Oh *Dad*," said Tamsin crossly. She hurried out of the front door and banged it shut behind her.

"I don't know," sighed Mr Langridge. "I still say she's too young to be doing this sort of thing."

"Oh *Richard*," said his wife. "Just this once, and only next door. Besides, it'll give her a taste of real responsibility."

"Well," said Mr Langridge, "all I can say is . . ."

"Oh *Richard*," said his wife.

Tamsin was by now knocking on the Plummers' front door. Mrs Plummer opened it, and asked her in. "It's good of you to help out, love," she said. "We're in a bit of a rush, so I'll just very quickly show you where everything is, and then we'll have to leave you to it."

Tamsin had never met Mrs Plummer before. She liked the way she didn't ask how old she was, or what school she went to, or what her favourite lessons were. Mrs Plummer got straight down to business, and Tamsin liked that.

Mrs Plummer took Tamsin's jacket and hung it up in the hall. Then she showed her where the toilet was, and how to switch on the TV in the living room. They went into the kitchen, and Mrs Plummer opened a large square biscuit tin that stood on the kitchen table.

"Brownies," she said. "Eat as many as you can. I made them this morning and they won't be nearly as nice tomorrow."

Tamsin peered into the tin at the dark, glistening rectangles, packed tightly together, side by side and end to end. With her eye, she singled out the biggest and best.

Mrs Plummer had moved away from the table, and was pointing out tea and coffee in a cupboard. "There's milk in here," she said, opening the fridge door. Tamsin couldn't see any milk bottles or cartons, but there were several large jugs, all brim-full.

"Goats' milk, of course," said Mrs Plummer. "Hope you don't mind. It tastes much better than cows', you know, and it's much better for you."

"Oh," said Tamsin. "Yes. Of course."

Mrs Plummer moved towards the kitchen door, but Tamsin stayed by the fridge. "Um, Mrs Plummer," she said. "Um, I was going to ask you if you'd have time . . ."

"Goodness me!" Mrs Plummer broke in. "I nearly forgot the most important thing. I nearly forgot to introduce the baby-sitter to the baby! Come on!"

There was no time for Tamsin to finish what she had wanted to say. She followed Mrs Plummer upstairs.

The bathroom door was ajar and, through it, Tamsin saw Mr Plummer in a string vest, shaving. He didn't stop what he was doing, but he threw out a sideways glance and said, "Hello, Tamsin," as they went past.

Mrs Plummer stopped outside a door with lots of stickers on it. The biggest sticker was a red and silver striped J, and next-biggest was a notice that said STRICTLY PRIVATE.

"Are you in bed, J?" Mrs Plummer called.

"Yes," said a voice, "but you're not allowed to come in. You're not allowed to bring the baby-sitter in."

Mrs Plummer opened the door and switched on the light. "Come in, Tamsin," she said. For a moment, Tamsin saw a small child, screwing up its eyes against the sudden brightness. Then the child flung the duvet over its head and disappeared.

"Don't be silly," said Mrs Plummer. "Come out from under there and say hello to Tamsin." The head appeared again, looking tousled, and the eyes, still squinting a little, stared grumpily.

"This is Tamsin Langridge from next door," said Mrs Plummer. "She's come to be here with you while Dad and I are out, like I explained."

"When are you coming back?"

"Soon," said Mrs Plummer. "Now, Tamsin, believe it or not -" she smiled "- this is James."

Tamsin couldn't think of anything to say, so she just mumbled, "Hello." James didn't say hello, but he said to his mother, "Go away. Leave me alone." Before she went, Mrs Plummer kissed him and said, "Good night, darling." And as she and Tamsin made their way back downstairs, they heard James calling, "Mumm-ee! Don't be out lo-ong!"

Mrs Plummer sat down on the sofa in the living room, and began rummaging through her handbag. She found a little bottle of scent and dabbed some on behind her ears. Then she found a lipstick and began putting that on, holding a miniature mirror up to her face.

Tamsin sat down in a big armchair and watched. Then, after a short silence,

"Um, er, Mrs Plummer," she said. "I was wondering, Mrs Plummer, if I could . . . if you'd have time – just quickly – to show me . . . to take me to see . . . Jemima?"

Mrs Plummer finished doing her lipstick and began saying, "Well, Tamsin, we are rather late, I'm afraid. Perhaps another time . . ." She glanced across at the armchair: a big armchair with a small girl, looking very disappointed, sitting on the edge of it. "Oh well, I suppose we're not that late. All right, love. Only you'll have to go with Derek – Mr Plummer, that is – because I don't want to mess up these shoes."

When Mr Plummer came downstairs and heard the plan, he didn't look as if he wanted to mess up *his* shoes, either, but he agreed to take Tamsin, all the same. He led the way out of the back door and down the garden.

The Plummers' garden was long and narrow. It was divided from the Langridges' by a solid wooden fence, too high to look over and too sturdy to peep through. Tamsin knew. She had often tried, but never managed, to see Jemima from the other side.

At the bottom of the Plummers' garden was a small enclosure made of sawn-up old doors, and inside the enclosure was a cosy-looking wooden shed with a proper door of its own. The shed door was fixed open with a bit of string

19

looped round the latch, and Tamsin could see straw spilling out over the threshold. She couldn't see right in because the doorway wasn't on the side of the shed that faced them as they came along the path.

Mr Plummer was telling Tamsin how he and Mrs Plummer had built the shed and the enclosure with their own hands. When he and Tamsin reached the enclosure, he wanted Tamsin to feel for herself how firm the posts were – but Tamsin hardly heard him. All her attention was fixed on the open doorway, and her ears were straining to pick up the slight rustling coming from inside the shed.

"Solid as a rock," Mr Plummer was saying. "Beautiful. Fit for a princess, this is. Yes –" he looked towards the doorway and spoke the rest of what he had to say to the face that had suddenly appeared there "– Yes, it's much too good for an ungrateful old goat like you!"

The goat stared calmly back at him, then half-closed her eyes, raised her head a little, and gave a husky, high-pitched bleat. Tamsin had often heard the sound before, through the fence.

"Jemima!" she called, and stretched out her hand over the top of one of the old doors. "Jemima! Jemima! Come on, Jemima, don't be shy!"

"Pooh!" said Mr Plummer, laughing. "Shy! *That* old rogue! That's a good one! No, she's just contrary. Always likes to do the opposite to what you want her to do."

Sure enough, Jemima made no move to come over to Tamsin, but went on looking out from the doorway, waiting to see what would happen next. She didn't even bleat again.

"Can I go in and stroke her?" asked Tamsin. "She won't bite, will she?"

"Bite? No, she won't bite. She's gentle enough. But time's getting on –" Mr Plummer looked at his watch "– and we'd best go back to the house now. Come another day, when things aren't such a rush."

On the way back, Mr Plummer talked about the finishing touches that still needed to be done on Jemima's shed.

"There's the door, for one thing," he said. "I've still got to make a proper catch to hold it open. It's nice for the old girl to have it open on warm nights like we're having at the moment, and that bit of string's no good at all. If there's the slightest breeze, then the string works off and the door swings to. Don't worry if you hear a bang, incidentally: that's what it'll be. The shed door. It sometimes wakes James, but he doesn't worry. He knows what it is by now."

When they got indoors again, they found Mrs Plummer eager to be off. While Mr Plummer went to find the car keys, she gave Tamsin some last-minute instructions. She told her that the electric kettle had to be switched off when it came to the boil, as the automatic switch had worn out. Also, she advised her not to have the TV turned up too loud, or it might wake James.

"And if he does wake, whatever you do – whatever he says – *don't* give him a brownie. He's already had all the bits that wouldn't fit into the tin, which is more than enough for one day. Help yourself – but no more for James, please."

After that, Mr and Mrs Plummer went, and Tamsin was left in charge, on her own.

At first she was fine because one of her favourite programmes was on TV. But when the programme was over, and the theme tune at the end had shut her out from the little half-an-hour, laugh-a-minute world, she began to feel nervous and jumpy. She'd promised herself a brownie after TV, but in the new, empty silence of the house she didn't feel like one. Besides, Mrs Plummer had probably memorized the exact size of each piece in the tin, and would see at once that Tamsin had gone for the biggest. No – better not have a brownie. And better not use the kettle, either, if it was on the blink. No tea or coffee, then.

Tamsin sat in the living room, keeping very still. She didn't want to make a noise because she didn't want to draw attention to herself as the only moving, noise-making thing in the house. But draw whose attention? Nobody's, of course. There was nobody there to see her or hear her – and yet she felt uncomfortable. Silly of her, but she couldn't help it.

Tamsin wished James would wake up and need a glass of water brought to him, or a bedtime story read. But there was silence from upstairs. She even tried a loud cough, in the hope of disturbing his sleep, but she only succeeded in frightening herself with her own explosion of sound.

At last, Tamsin could bear it no longer. She knew exactly where she wanted to be, and it wasn't here in the house. James didn't need her, did he? Besides, she wasn't exactly going to be leaving the premises. She got up and made a dash for the back door.

Night had fallen since Tamsin's trip to the bottom of the garden with Mr Plummer. But the moon was full, so she had no difficulty in seeing how to unbolt the gate of the goat enclosure, let herself in and bolt the gate behind her again. The shed itself was a different matter: although the loop of string held the door wide open, she could see nothing inside but blackness. She hesitated in the doorway and then, from the back of the shed, there was a bleat. It wasn't like the sound Tamsin had heard earlier, with Mr Plummer. This time it was as if Jemima had bleated with her mouth shut. The sound was a bit like someone with a blocked nose trying to suppress a giggle – or like an engine that won't start, just muttering before it lapses into silence.

Tamsin looked towards the sound and dimly made out two white stripes at about knee-level. They must be the stripes on either side of Jemima's face. The rest of Jemima's body, Tamsin knew from her daylight visit, was a rich, chocolate brown. Dark as the darkness in the shed, it remained invisible now.

Tamsin stepped inside the shed, which was just high enough for her to stand up in, and moved towards Jemima. Again Jemima bleated, and this time Tamsin was sure she understood what the sound meant. Jemima wasn't questioning anything, but just letting Tamsin know that she knew about her. Tamsin understood that she was to come in if she were coming, and settle down if she were staying, and stop disturbing the peace and quiet of the night. So she went right up to Jemima, who was lying in the straw, and sat down next to her.

Tamsin had always liked animals, but had never had the chance to get to know one. Being there alone with Jemima was better than anything she had ever imagined. She felt so safe and so calm, breathing in the warm darkness of the shed, that smelt mostly of hay and a little of milk.

Gently, with her fingertips, she stroked Jemima's smooth flank. Jemima looked round and sniffed Tamsin's hand. Then she sniffed Tamsin's T-shirt. Then she took Tamsin's T-shirt in her mouth and gave a sharp tug.

"Oi!" said Tamsin. "Don't! Let go of it!" But Jemima held on and wouldn't let go till Tamsin batted her muzzle with her hand. Jemima's muzzle felt soft and velvety. She didn't seem in the least bit flustered or upset by her telling-off.

Tamsin thought it would be nice to snuggle down with her head resting on Jemima's side. She tried it, but Jemima once again looked round and this time took hold of a mouthful of Tamsin's hair.

"Ouch!" squeaked Tamsin, and jerked her head away. Jemima still didn't seem taken aback. She breathed heavily and evenly, as before, and Tamsin was content to listen to her and stroke her side.

And then, suddenly . . .

BANG!

Tamsin gasped with the shock of the noise, and even Jemima gave a start. It had been like a single hand-clap, though the hands that clapped had, by the sound of them, been made of wood. Of course! The shed door! It must have slammed shut, as Mr Plummer had warned Tamsin that it might.

The darkness inside the shed was now absolute, but Tamsin got up and felt her way over to the door. She fumbled for the latch, but couldn't find it. She tried pushing the door and, yes, it definitely was latched fast: she could hear the latch rattle when she pushed. She felt again for a handle, and got a splinter in her finger. More cautiously, she felt all round the edges of the door for a bolt, a keyhole, anything – but there was nothing. The latch, Tamsin realized as she sucked her hurt finger, must have been made to be lifted only from the outside. She herself, on the inside, was trapped.

What would Mr and Mrs Plummer say, when they got back and found their baby-sitter at the bottom of the garden with the goat? One thing was for sure: they'd never ask her to baby-sit again.

If Tamsin had been on her own, she'd probably have cried, but as it was, she didn't want to worry Jemima. From her corner, Jemima bleated, and Tamsin felt that she must stop fussing at once. She shuffled back to sit down where she'd sat before and, as before, began stroking Jemima with the tips of her fingers. She soon forgot about the splinter: the soreness in that finger seemed to fade as she stroked. Neck, flank, and all along the long, nobbly backbone. When she stroked Jemima's head, she used her whole palm and pressed quite hard, because the head was hard and bony. It was especially hard and bony on top, where Jemima's horns would have been if she'd had any.

The bit that Tamsin liked best was the underside of Jemima's neck, close to where it met her jawbone. There, dangling down, were two funny little tassels, each about the size of the top half of Tamsin's middle finger. They were covered in soft fur, and didn't seem to have any bones in them. Gently, Tamsin pulled and rubbed and rolled them between her finger and thumb. Jemima didn't try to stop her, and so Tamsin knew – there in the hay-scented darkness – that it must feel nice.

After a while, Jemima burped. The sound was like the pipes in a house at night, gurgling softly to themselves when everyone else is asleep. Then she began munching something. She was chewing the cud.

Listening to Jemima chewing, Tamsin felt happier than she'd felt for a long time. So what if everything was ruined for the future? Here and now, she had what she wanted.

And then Tamsin got her second shock that night. Another noise, but not the kind that makes you jump, as the banging door had been. It was a noise that made Tamsin feel stiff and cold and shivery. It came from outside the shed. Just outside. It was the noise of somebody doing something out there. Drawing back the bolt of the enclosure gate, opening the gate, shutting it again.

Jemima had stopped chewing, to listen. Tamsin's heart, pounding strongly, seemed to be trying to force its way up into her throat. Who could it be out there? Mr and Mrs Plummer weren't due back for ages.

Tamsin listened to the latch of the shed door being lifted. With one hand still laid on Jemima, she closed her eyes.

The door opened. Tamsin kept her eyes closed. She waited for something horrible, but nothing happened. Instead, Jemima bleated. 'Oh *you*,' she seemed to say. Then she burped and began chewing again.

Tamsin opened her eyes and saw, framed in the moonlit doorway,

"James!"

He stood there in his pyjamas, not looking afraid or anxious or even surprised. Just a bit crotchety that the baby-sitter hadn't been where she ought to have been.

"Oh *James*!" said Tamsin.

"Can I have a brownie?" said James.

PEDALLING AIR

Something funny was happening to Paul Peck. He was losing his touch. It was like watching a rabbit in a snare, thought Tamsin, as she watched him getting put into detention by teachers that he used to be able to handle. The more things went wrong, the more Paul struggled – and the more he struggled, the wronger things went. Tamsin didn't like to think of how the rabbit ended up. A dead thing, strangled and jerking at the end of a wire.

It began at school the next Monday. Paul hadn't seen anyone since Friday, when he'd said he didn't want to go round to Greg's.

"Wotcha, Pedaller!" Jessie called across the classroom, as they waited for their home economics teacher to arrive.

Paul took no notice. There was no reason for him to recognize that as his name.

"Oi, Pecky!" called Jess. "Pecky Pedaller!"

He looked round then. "What you on about, Jessie Lawson? What d'you mean?"

"Don't you know?" said Jessie. "Don't you know your name? Well, you know it now – and you'd better get used to it."

"You're nuts, Lawson," said Paul, but he looked nervous. "Loony Lawson."

Jessie ignored that. "Well," she said, "if you don't know about it, you can ask Tamsin. She knows because it was her idea."

Jessie nudged Tamsin and giggled. Tamsin giggled too, but she wished Jess hadn't said that, and she hoped Paul wouldn't ask her to explain. It was all so stupid.

26

But Paul couldn't leave it alone.

"All right then, Tamsin," he said. "Go on. Let's hear it from Tamsin Clever-Clever Langridge."

Tamsin went on giggling with Jessie. She pretended she couldn't stop. Jessie probably really did think it was funny, but Tamsin just wanted to put off explaining to Paul what had happened on Friday. The trouble was, she realized, that the longer they laughed and made out it was so funny, the less funny it would seem when Paul finally got it out of her. And that was why, the longer they laughed, the more she wanted never never to have to tell. For once, she wished that Mrs Flinch would come in and start the needlework lesson.

And Mrs Flinch did come – just as Paul was about to say something more.

"Quiet, please!" said Mrs Flinch. "Tamsin and Jessie, please be quiet." Mrs Flinch was one teacher you definitely couldn't answer back. Everybody knew that. There were secret ways of having a laugh in double needlework – like revving up your sewing machine or changing the stitch size on somebody else's when they weren't looking – but you couldn't hope to enjoy any part of the lesson if Mrs Flinch suspected anything was up. Suspect: that was her favourite word. "I *suspect* you'll need to stitch that twice over . . ." "I *suspect* you're not paying attention . . ." You could be sure Mrs Flinch would never see the funny side of anything, so you might as well not waste your breath on trying to get anything going with her. When Mrs Flinch said be quiet, you were quiet, and that was all there was to it.

But now, suddenly, it was as if Paul had forgotten all that. In the silence that followed Mrs Flinch's entrance, he said quite loudly and clearly,

"Come on, Tamsin. What were you going to say?"

Everyone looked at him. Mrs Flinch looked at him. But Paul just looked at Tamsin.

"Paul," said Mrs Flinch, "didn't you hear me? I said I wanted quiet. If Tamsin's got something interesting to say, then she can share it with the class. Now Tamsin, have you got something to tell us?"

"No, she hasn't," said Paul. "But she's got something to

tell *me*. Haven't you, Tamsin?"

"Paul, what is the matter with you? You can start behaving yourself this instant – or you can get out of my classroom."

Mrs Flinch paused, testing the silence. Then, "Thank you," she said. "Now perhaps we can begin work. Will you all get out the face flannels that you began hemming last week."

There was a scraping of chairs and a shuffling of feet and a burst of chatter, and everyone got up to fetch their needlework from the cupboard. Tamsin got up with the rest, but she felt Paul's eyes following her. Paul sat still, staring hard. Then, not shouting, but speaking loudly enough to be heard above all the noise, he said,

"Stuff face flannels! I want to know what Tamsin's got to say." He looked odd. Sort of desperate. "I – need – to know."

Mrs Flinch had frozen at the first words. Immediately after the last, she melted – but only to explode.

"How dare you! How dare you, Paul Peck! Get out!"

It was the first time Paul had ever been sent out of a classroom. As he walked to the door, he looked as if he might be about to cry – but that wasn't because of Mrs Flinch. True, he'd lost where he had always won before – but then, in a way, this time he hadn't really been playing. Everyone had realized that there'd been something different about Paul's outspokenness this time. He had behaved as if Mrs Flinch simply hadn't been there. His mind had been on something else: another, bigger game, that he knew, as soon as he was called a name he didn't understand, that he was beginning to lose.

After the needlework lesson, and for the next few days, Tamsin kept out of Paul's way as much as she could. She dreaded being cornered by him and having to tell how she'd said all that about the dead, pedalling hen just to protect herself. If anyone had been a chicken that day, it certainly wasn't Paul.

But as it turned out, Tamsin needn't have worried. After that first attempt, Paul seemed to give up hope of ever getting to the bottom of his mysterious name. Pecky Pedaller, The name stuck, although those who knew almost forgot how it had come about. Pedaller. It stuck like tar and feathers, thought Tamsin. The feathers of a white hen.

Paul might have given up on where the name had come from, but he wasn't giving up the whole game. It was a game you never realized you were playing till you started to lose. Desperately, he tried to win back his place amongst Greg and Jessie's lot. Desperately, he tried to play the joker as he had used to do. But his very desperation made him heavy-handed. Every single day that week he spent his lunch break in detention, writing out, five hundred times, 'I must not be rude to teachers' or 'I must learn to keep my mouth shut'. Nobody cheered the daring that led up to the detentions, because it was a mad sort of daring. At first the class just listened to it and stared. By Wednesday they were sneering at Paul for a failure. By Friday they were ignoring him because they'd seen it all before, and they were bored.

It was hardly surprising, now, that Paul never went round to Greg's loft. When he slipped home quickly after school, nobody tried to stop him any more. And even if he'd hung around, no one from the loft gang would have asked him to go with them.

Tamsin had gone to the loft as usual on Monday and Tuesday. Now, in Friday's diary lesson, she prepared to write up her week. Accuracy, she remembered, was one of the most important things in a journal, and – accurately speaking – the week began with Monday. So she hurriedly wrote about Monday and Tuesday – and Greg's loft and Greg's loft. When she got to Wednesday, she paused for a moment before writing anything down. Wednesday was when the week had really begun.

'After school,' wrote Tamsin, 'I cycled straight back to Whenock.' Back to Whenock, yes, but not back home. She wrote about how she'd turned in at the Plummers' front gate instead of her own, and how she'd knocked on the Plummers' front door and asked whether she could be taken to see Jemima. Mrs Plummer had given her the ragged outer leaf of a cabbage, and taken her down to the bottom of the garden. And Tamsin had fed the cabbage leaf to Jemima, and stroked her as if she were touching goat for the first time.

The next day – Thursday – Tamsin had again gone to see Jemima straight from school. Mrs Plummer had given her a whole handful of cabbage leaves this time, and allowed her to go by herself to the goat enclosure. She'd stayed there, watching Jemima, stroking her and talking to her, until it was time to be getting home for tea.

All this Tamsin wrote in her diary. When she came to Friday, she wrote,

'I am going to see Jemima again today. I have saved her my apple from lunch. I am sure she will like apple, seeing as she likes old, tough cabbage leaves.'

Tamsin paused, wondering whether Jemima would be able to open her mouth wide enough to get the apple in whole. She had eaten the cabbage leaves quickly and easily, drawing each one into her mouth like somebody jerkily pulling a sheet of newspaper in through a letterbox. But an apple might be more difficult for her. Perhaps Tamsin would have to bite chunks off it herself, and offer them one by one.

Almost without thinking, Tamsin's eyes went back over the last sentence she had written. Word by word, letter by letter. '. . . old, tough cabbage leaves.' The 'o' in 'tough' gapped at the top, but the one at the beginning of 'old' was a complete ring, a near-perfect circle. In her imagination, Tamsin climbed inside – where it was already half an hour after the end of school and she was already in the enclosure with Jemima. She was feeding apple to Jemima, and gently stroking Jemima's neck with the fingers of her free hand.

"Oh no you don't!" Tamsin looked up quickly, afraid for a moment that Mr Lively must have seen her slipping away. But he hadn't been speaking to her at all. It was just that he'd noticed someone at the back of the room unwisely closing her exercise book – five minutes before the lesson was due to finish.

"I want everyone working till quarter to four," he said sternly. "Any books closed before then will each add on five minutes to that time – for everyone."

The way Mr Lively said 'books' made the word sound like 'box'. He always said 'box' instead of 'books', just as he told you to wash out your 'years' instead of your 'ears'. Even when he raised his voice, it was always somehow soft – and people liked him all the more because of it. Nobody ever thought of laughing at Mr Lively's accent.

The girl who had closed her book now opened it again, but another book was closed – loudly – as soon as Mr Lively had finished speaking.

"Right, Paul," he said at once, "that's five minutes extra work you've just earned for the class. Well done, lad!"

The whole class groaned, and someone said bitterly, "Thanks a lot, Pedaller!"

Paul said, "But sir, that's not fair. What've I done wrong?"

"*Ten* minutes extra work!" replied Mr Lively. "Nobody goes till five to four!"

Everyone glowered at Paul. He said, "But I didn't do anything."

"Paul," said Mr Lively, "when I say no books closed till quarter to four – and you close yours before quarter to, then you know and I know that something's wrong. If you can't see that, then I advise you to get yourself some spectacles."

"But sir," said Paul, "I only closed my *book*. I haven't even got a *box* . . ."

He trailed off. Mr Lively looked dark, like a storm cloud about to break. He stood up and pointed a finger at Paul, and it was as if the cloud had blotted out the sun. Then,

"TOO FAR!" he thundered. "You've gone too far this time, lad. Come out here and stand beside my desk."

Paul evidently felt he had gone too far, and did as he was told.

"You'll stand there till quarter *past* four," continued Mr Lively, "and by that time you'll have thought how to word an abject apology. Make it good, lad, or you'll be explaining your behaviour to the Head on Monday."

Nobody had seen Mr Lively like that before. Everyone felt a bit scared. When the outburst had ended, they were all glad to be able to concentrate on their diaries once more.

Standing at the front of the classroom, with nothing to concentrate on, Paul felt awkward and uncomfortable. Rather than looking out over the rest of the class, he looked down at the floor. But it wasn't the floor that met his gaze. Tamsin and Jessie sat in the middle of the front row, and Paul found that when he looked down, his eyes fell on Tamsin's desk. He was actually standing very close to it, and his view of her open exercise book was perfect – except for being upside-down. Paul began to amuse himself by trying to read the upside-down writing. It wasn't that difficult really. He'd soon read the whole of the left-hand page – which was the last part of Wednesday's entry and the first part of Thursday's. He read on now with interest. On the right-hand page was the rest of Thursday and the whole of Friday. Paul had read the lot before Mr Lively announced the end of the lesson.

People spoke in hushed voices to their neighbours as they put their things away and got up to go.

"Blimey!" Jess said to Tamsin. "I don't half need an hour round Greg's. Feel sort of jumpy . . . Come on, let's hurry."

"I'm baby-sitting for next door again," said Tamsin. "Got to be there at half four, like yesterday, to give the kid his tea." She made a face. "Wish I could come, but I don't want to mess up this job."

Jess was about to argue, when her attention was diverted.

"You keep your nose out, Nosy Parker Pedaller. Give over listening and mind your own business."

Paul shrugged and stepped back a bit. He looked out of the window. Jessie and Tamsin left the classroom.

Through the window, Paul could see the two girls making off for the bike sheds. They were soon hidden from sight by one of the mobile classrooms, but he could imagine just what they'd be doing. Reaching their bikes, unlocking them, wheeling them to the school gates. Greg, with one or two others, would be waiting there. Jess would join the group and lead it, with Greg, into Swinston High Street. Tamsin would cycle off in the other direction, out of Swinston, towards Whenock.

While Mr Lively was putting chalk away and banging about in the stock cupboard, Paul was thinking. Tamsin would be well on her way to Whenock by now. Paul was thinking hard, but when Mr Lively asked him for his apology, he was taken by surprise. He'd forgotten all about it.

GRAVESTONE GHOST

"Funny things, goats," said Mr Langridge, through a mouthful of cauliflower cheese. He only ever spoke with his mouth full when he was really hungry – and he was really hungry this evening, because he'd been to a meeting of the Parish Council that had gone on longer than usual.

Tamsin and Mrs Langridge had got fed up with waiting, and had started supper without him. They were on their pudding already.

"Goats aren't funny," said Tamsin, sucking a peach stone.

"Don't talk with your mouth full," said her father.

"I . . ."

"Leave it!" said her mother.

They went on eating in silence.

Mr Langridge reached behind him to the cutlery drawer, and fished out a teaspoon. He used it to scoop up the last, rather watery traces of cheese sauce that had been too runny for the prongs of his fork. Then he put the spoon and his knife and fork together, and sighed contentedly.

"Fussy about food, apparently," he said.

"Apparently *not*, I'd say," said Mrs Langridge, looking at her husband's empty plate. "Richard, what *are* you talking about? *Who's* fussy about food?"

"Goats," said Mr Langridge. "They won't touch their food once it's fallen on the ground, if the ground's at all dirty – which is funny, because you tend to think of goats as eating anything and everything."

"Who's been talking to you about goats, then?"

"Oh, not just to me," said Mr Langridge. "She was telling the whole meeting. Lisa Plummer from next door. Wants

33

permission to graze her goat on the rough patch at the bottom of the churchyard. Apparently, the place where they keep this goat gets a bit mucky, and the thing would eat better – and be better generally – if they could tether it away from home."

"What did you say to her, Dad?" asked Tamsin.

"Well, I said it was funny, because you tend to think of goats as . . ."

"No, no," Tamsin interrupted. "I mean, what did the Council say? What did the Council decide?"

"Well, Mr Raven said he'd once been butted by a goat and Pat Coxall said goats smell . . ."

"They don't," said Tamsin.

"That's as maybe," said Mr Langridge. "As Mrs Clayton pointed out, nobody would smell anything anyway, right down at the far end of the churchyard. And Mr Raven said Mrs Clayton wouldn't be so keen if she'd ever been on the wrong end of a goat's horns. And Mrs Clayton said she wasn't 'keen', she just didn't see any harm in it – and what was the 'wrong' end of a goat's horns anyway? And Mr Raven said the sharp end. And everyone laughed. So, seeing the way things were going, I thought I might as well . . ."

"Dad!" broke in Tamsin. "You didn't! You didn't go along with them! They don't know a thing about goats and neither do you and Jemima hasn't got horns anyway!" She was practically shouting.

"Tamsie, do shut up," said her father. "I was just going to tell you that what I said was that since Mr Haines went into semi-retirement, he hasn't had much time for the churchyard, and the bit at the bottom, where he can't get the mower, has gone quite wild. I said we could do with a mowing machine on four legs."

"Oh."

"And Lisa Plummer said there was nothing like a goat for keeping down the rough stuff. And, one way or another, all except Mr Raven, we came round to agreeing that she could tether the thing there whenever she liked."

"Oh Dad," said Tamsin, "that's great."

Mrs Langridge, who had been looking at the paper and

listening with only half an ear, now said, "What's the big deal, Tamsin? Why all the fuss? And who's Jemima?"

"Jemima's the goat, Mum," said Tamsin. "Mrs Plummer showed her to me when I went baby-sitting that time. Her enclosure was really small and she'd worn away all the grass in it – so I was just thinking how nice it would be for her in the churchyard." Tamsin turned towards Mr Langridge again. "When's Mrs Plummer going to start taking her there, Dad?"

"Tomorrow, so she said. If the weather's fine. But she'll have taken it home again by the time you get back. She milks it at five thirty, apparently, so she'll never leave it there much after five."

Tamsin didn't say anything.

"Now if you didn't insist on hanging around after school every day with Jessie Lawson and that Greg of hers, you might . . ."

"Oh Richard," said Mrs Langridge. "Don't start on about that again. Please."

The next day, the weather was fine. In fact it was beautiful – and Tamsin cycled off after school as quickly as she could. Jessie didn't try to persuade her to go round to Greg's: she'd got used to this business of Tamsin's making tea for the little boy next door. Last week, Tamsin had gone with the others to Greg's loft on only two days out of the five.

Tamsin reached Whenock in record time. She turned up Church Street as usual, but cycled past both her own house and the Plummers'. The church stood at the far end of the row of council houses that began at the Swinston Road junction.

Tamsin got off her bike and wheeled it through the little iron gate of the churchyard. She crunched with it up the gravel path, and leaned it against the outside of the church porch. Then she followed the path round the side of the church.

The sun was shining warmly on the dark green yew trees and the grey gravestones and the bright white daisies and little blue flowers in the grass. It was all very quiet, except for the

35

birds, and Tamsin stood still for a moment, almost forgetting why she had come. Then she heard Jemima bleating to her, and she left the path and hurried off towards the sound.

You could see why Mr Haines had given up on the bit of the churchyard that was now allowed to be Jemima's. It was a sort of gravestone dumping ground, where the stones that broke or fell over in other parts of the churchyard were brought and left: over the decades, tidied out of the way. Against the end wall, pieces of masonry were heaped like a rockery, but elsewhere they were strewn about at random, nestling singly or in groups in the dry, wispy couch-grass.

Ivy and couch-grass had taken over here. The grass was long because Mr Haines didn't dare run his mower over it – for fear of catching the blades on a piece of stone. And he hadn't got the time now to go at it with a pair of shears. He had mown as near the rough patch as he thought safe, making a straight line across the width of the churchyard, where the short grass stopped and the long grass and romping ivy began.

Jemima was standing on top of a tomb that was like a great solid, stone table. At one time – a long time ago – the bit of the churchyard now on the overgrown side of Mr Haines's boundary line must have been no less tidy than the rest of the place. It had had its own graves and its own stones to mark them – and these stones were still here. They stood (though often lop-sidedly) among the dumped fragments (which lay flat). By far the grandest of the standing stones was the great solid table from where Jemima now looked down on Tamsin's approach.

Tamsin knew her well enough not to expect Jemima to come to meet her. When she called her name, it wasn't a call for her to come, but just a greeting. "Mima, Mima! Hello Mima!"

Jemima watched with interest as Tamsin picked her way carefully through the higher-than-knee-high grass, flinging out her arms like a large, awkward bird whenever she stepped on a hidden piece of stone and was thrown off balance. When Tamsin arrived at the table-like tomb, she had to reach up to stroke Jemima. Jemima's coat was warm from the sun, and her belly was rounded from the ivy and grass that she'd been feasting on.

Now that Tamsin was with her, Jemima no longer seemed interested. Her ears, which had been pricked before, now flicked about lazily, batting away the flies that landed on her face. Tamsin tickled the base of Jemima's left ear and then, with her fingertips, traced the line of the jawbone down from the ear to the two tassels dangling at the throat. Jemima held still, half-closing her eyes, while Tamsin rubbed the tassels, each in turn, between finger and thumb. Then Tamsin left the table tomb for another stone, a little way off.

The new stone (but it wasn't new: it looked very, very old) was an upright tablet. Tamsin sat down on a mat of couch-grass at its foot, her back flat against it. Couch-grass prickled the backs of her knees. She picked a daisy and began singing, "Mima, Mima, give me your answer, do . . ." She sang softly, as if to herself, and looked down at the flower which she twirled round in her fingers.

Tamsin knew that the only way to get Jemima to come to her was to make Jemima think that she didn't especially want her to come. Jemima had watched Tamsin intently as she left and sat down and picked the daisy. Intently, she listened to the singing. Then she stepped to one end of the flat tomb top, where a higgledy-piggledy heap of masonry made a sort of ramp to the ground. With a sudden, jerky but sure-footed rush, she was down in the couch-grass, sniffing about and nibbling this and that. Absent-mindedly sniffing and nibbling, she moved off. Absent-mindedly sniffing and nibbling, she just happened to end up right by Tamsin, sitting against the gravestone and singing to herself in the warm, beaming, half-past-four sun.

Jemima lay down beside Tamsin, so close that her flank pressed against Tamsin's leg. Tamsin just happened to put her arm round Jemima's neck. Still she sang, but now the song was hardly more than a murmur. She felt for Jemima's tassels and gently tugged and rubbed each one. Jemima burped and began to chew the cud. Tamsin smiled.

The two of them stayed like that until they heard someone coming. Someone coming from the direction of the church, behind them. Jemima heard first, and stopped chewing. She didn't turn her head, but her ears strained back to listen. Then Tamsin heard, and she did twist round.

It was James Plummer. He stomped resolutely over the rough ground, his arms now thrown up above his head, now plunging down to anchor him to any piece of stone that tried to trip him up. He was soon standing in front of them, and the first to speak was Jemima. She gave him her chugging, chuckling bleat, and then began chewing again. He said, "Hello, Jemima."

"Hello, James," said Tamsin. "What're you doing here?"

"Hello, Tamsin Language," said James. "What're *you* doing here?" He'd just come through a phase of not being able to say his 'r's, and still had lapses with some particular words. He always said Tamsin's surname in the old way, because then it was a proper word with a proper meaning, and James liked things to make sense. "Tamsin Language," he said again. "What're you doing here?"

It never occurred to Tamsin that James might have as much, or more, right to be with Jemima as she had. James obviously didn't love Jemima as Tamsin loved her – he hardly seemed to care about her at all – and that made her more Tamsin's goat than his. Also, Tamsin was irritated by James's habit of calling her (Tamsin) by her first and second names together. Sometimes he even addressed her as 'Tamsin Language from next door'. So now she ignored his question and, in a rather grown-up voice, asked him another.

"Does your mummy know you're here?"

"Course," said James. "Mummy sent me. Mummy said to make sure Jemima hadn't wound up all her chain and to tell her she'd be along soon to take her home for milking."

He looked at Jemima and then at Tamsin, and evidently felt too shy to give Jemima her message straight out. He skipped that half of his instructions and set about attending to the other half instead.

Jemima was tethered by a long chain, which was clipped at one end to her collar, and at the other end joined to a heavy iron stake hammered into the ground. Part of the chain's length had got wound round the stake, and James now began to unwind it, lifting it with both hands over the top of the stake again and again. When he'd finished, the bit he'd just unwound lay in a heap of links on the ground. He came back to Tamsin and Jemima, and sat down on a piece of stone, facing them.

"Mummy said to wait here for her," he said. "What're you playing?"

"I'm not playing anything," said Tamsin. "Not everything has to be a game, you know, James." Honestly, what a baby he was!

"Yes, you are – and I know what. So there! You're playing hide-and-seek." He paused. "Can I play?"

"For God's sake, don't be so silly, James. You can *see* I'm not playing hide-and-seek. And even if I was, I definitely wouldn't let you join in."

"Don't lie," said James grimly. "Don't pretend you're not playing, because I know you *are*. You've been seeking, but now you've given up because you can't find him."

"You're a nutter," said Tamsin. "Find who?"

"Liar!" shouted James. "Your friend who's hiding, of course – back there by the church."

Suddenly Tamsin felt stiff and panicky, like you feel in bed when you hear a creak on the stairs. In bed, Tamsin always wriggled right down under the covers and stayed still until the thing on the stairs was forced to admit, by making no further move, that it was nothing at all. But this was different.

"James," she said quietly, "what was – what was my friend doing? Where was he exactly?"

"Cheat!" snapped James. Tamsin could tell he was so furious with her that he might refuse to say anything further.

"Come on," she said. "Please."

James spoke to Tamsin one more time during the next ten minutes – and then Mrs Plummer came to collect Jemima, and they all left the churchyard together. It was a little while after Tamsin had said please that James said, "Anyway, you're stupid, because I told you before what he was doing: hiding." The birds went on chirruping and chattering, and the sun went on shining, but Tamsin felt cold.

"Like I said," James went on, "he was hiding over there." He pointed. "Behind a gravestone. Watching you."

LETTERS

By the end of the following week, Tamsin was telling herself that there had been nobody watching her in the churchyard, after all. James had been making it up. She went every day now, but never saw anyone lurking there. James often joined her – and he never mentioned hide-and-seek again. He would be pestering her with more questions, wouldn't he, if he suspected that there was – or ever really had been – a secret game going on?

So Tamsin told herself that there had been nobody watching her that day. And she might have believed it, but for her diary.

Mr Lively had said that the class must write truthfully about their experiences and feelings, and that was what Tamsin always did. It felt good to write things as they really were, after she'd led other people to see them in different – other – ways. She was sometimes uneasy about what she said to Jess, to her mother and father, even to Mrs Plummer. But what she said in her diary seemed to make all that OK. Only Mr Lively ever saw her diary, and he had nothing to do with anything outside school or anything that mattered.

Once, after that first day in the churchyard, Tamsin had looked back at the page in her diary where it was written down. She wanted to be able to laugh and say, 'Oh, how silly I was!' But instead she found she felt frightened all over again. In the diary, her fear and her certain belief in a hidden watcher was fresh and real. And what you feel at the time of something happening is usually worth more than your feelings later on, after you've plumped them up with common sense, and made them all nice and comfortable.

She'd quickly shut the diary again, and tried hard to forget about what had happened that day and what she'd felt – and *what she'd felt had happened*. It was all there, written down, but she had to pretend it wasn't, or she'd never have dared to go into the churchyard again.

And Tamsin *had* to go into the churchyard – every day – because, every day now, that was where Jemima was.

It was much better, no longer having to knock on the Plummers' front door and ask permission to walk down their garden. Not that Mr or Mrs Plummer had ever been unfriendly – and they'd certainly never refused her permission – but she'd just felt awkward: always asking exactly the same thing, in exactly the same words, when the front door opened. It was that that had kept her away, some days. Some days, she'd still gone round to Greg's loft.

Yes, now that Jemima was tethered in the churchyard, it was much, much better. Every day, after school, Tamsin could cycle straight round to the churchyard to see her.

Most days, James turned up, too. Tamsin wasn't clear exactly what his reason was, except that he seemed to like routine. He never said much and Tamsin put up with him. In a funny sort of way, James was a bit like Jemima. Jemima never questioned Tamsin's coming, day after day: she seemed to have taken the first day as a pattern for all the days that followed. And – after the first day – James never questioned the goings-on in the churchyard, either.

Although it was always the same there, Tamsin never got tired of things the way they were. There was always plenty to write in Friday's diary lesson. For one thing, she was keeping a record of the time it took each day for Jemima to come over and lie down beside her, wherever she'd chosen to sit, within the circle that Jemima's chain allowed. The time depended on so many things: whether Jemima was lying down or standing up when Tamsin arrived; how far from Tamsin she was; how many tempting plants she stopped to nibble on her way. Once, over three days, the time got steadily less and less, and Tamsin dreamed of a day when Jemima would come trotting towards her straight away, and lay her head in her

41

lap. But Jemima just wasn't like that. On the fourth day, she took so long to make up her mind to come that Tamsin thought she wasn't going to bother at all. She did come in the end, and then it didn't seem to matter that she'd messed up Tamsin's precious calculations.

Tamsin was also noting down the names of the wild flowers that she found at the bottom of the churchyard. Apart from daisy and buttercup, there was quite a bit of bramble and dog rose there. One day, she found a cluster of deep purple, velvety flowers, rather like miniature pansies. She looked them up in a book in the school library, and found that they were violets.

Violets! They weren't at all what she would have thought of as violet in colour: nothing like the pencil marked 'violet' in her coloured pencil set, and certainly nothing like the eyeshadow called *Violent Violet* which Jessie had worn to the Valentine's Disco last term. It just went to show how much better it was to see things for yourself and make up your own mind about them, rather than going along with other people's ideas of what was what.

The violet day was good, but the day that Tamsin found the letters was even better. A real red-letter day, her mother would have called it. Only Tamsin's letters weren't red: they were a soft, dark grey. Probably, they were made of lead.

Tamsin found the letters when she was sitting by a gravestone that was new to her. Mrs Plummer had tethered Jemima on a fresh patch, where the grass was dense and untrodden, and when Tamsin came round the side of the church, she could see at once that today wasn't going to be a good day for her timing project. Jemima was lying on a gravestone that had fallen flat, and she looked full and fat and blissfully happy. She greeted Tamsin with a bleat that was hardly more than a husky sigh.

Tamsin picked her way over to Jemima, and rubbed her tassels and stroked her sleek, bulging sides. Then she went a little way off, to a small, plain-looking gravestone that had slumped slightly forward – though not enough to spoil it as a back-rest. She sat down in the grass at the foot of the stone, and leant against it.

She started timing. It was important that she shouldn't let Jemima know she was actually waiting for her to get up and come over. If Jemima thought that, then she'd never ever come. As Mr Plummer had said in the beginning, Jemima was contrary. So now Tamsin busied herself with other things: anything that had nothing to do with Jemima. She looked for daisies to make a daisy-chain, but couldn't find any within reach. (She couldn't move from the spot she'd chosen to sit on: that was one of the rules.) She tried making a buttercup-chain out of the buttercups close to hand, but their stalks were too tough and stringy. Then, just to prove to Jemima that she really wasn't the slightest bit interested, Tamsin turned her back on her: she shuffled round on her bottom to face the stone she'd been leaning against.

This gravestone was different from any of the others Tamsin had looked at, because instead of there being writing carved into it, there was writing stuck on to it. Each letter was made of a dull, blackish stuff, and had been fixed on separately, like numbers on a front door. It was easy to read the writing because the letters stood out dark against the pale grey stone. This is what it said:

IN L VING EMORY OF

WIF OF JOSIAH L VING
BOR 30th EPT   BER 1779
DIED 2 th   ARCH 184

E LORD GAVE AND TH   LO
H TH TAKEN WAY. BLE SED
BE TH   NAME OF THE L RD.

At least, that's what it said when Tamsin first read it. Just as she reached *E LORD GAVE*, something quite astounding happened. Not astounding like a brilliant fireworks display. More like a swallow flying high over an enormous football crowd; and the swallow shedding one, wispy feather; and the feather floating and eddying down and down and down; and landing – on the knuckles of your hand as you throw your arms up above your head to cheer a goal.

As Tamsin was reading *E LORD GAVE*, something small and dark and quite heavy dropped, without a sound, past the *E* of *GAVE* and down into the ivy at the foot of the stone. When she looked up, this is what the writing on the stone said:

IN L VING   EMORY OF

ANN   ARIA

WIF OF JOSIAH L VING
BOR   30th EPT   BER 1779
DIED 2 th   ARCH 184

E LORD GAVE AND TH   LO
H TH TAKEN WAY. BLE SED
BE TH   NAME OF THE L RD.

Tamsin worked out afterwards that what had happened had only happened twenty-one times before. Only twenty-one times since eighteen-forty-something, when Ann Maria had died and the gravestone had been erected. And on the twenty-second time, Tamsin had been right there and seen it. If she'd been touching the stone – if she'd stretched out her fingers to *GAVE* as her eyes had, for a moment, rested there to read – the *M* might have fallen into her hand.

She parted the ivy to look for the letter. It seemed meant for her. After all, it had waited for her ever since eighteen-forty-. . . Eighteen-forty-*one*! Peering through the leaves, she had not seen the *M*, but a *1*. She picked it up. It had certainly come from the writing on the stone, because it was exactly the same colour as the stuck-on letters. There were two little pegs on the back of it, like the points of tiny nails, and Tamsin noticed for the first time that, wherever there was a letter missing from the gravestone, there were two or three little holes in its place. She tried pressing the back of her *1*

44

into the stone just after *184*. The pegs fitted the holes there, and when she took her hand away, the stone said that Ann Maria had died in 1841. Only it still said *ANN ARIA*, of course. Tamsin carefully unpegged the *I* and laid it on the ground, to one side; then she went to work again in amongst the ivy, searching for the *M*.

In the end, she stripped off the ivy altogether and threw it away. Underneath the blanket it had made was a bed of speckled, pinky-brown granite chips, thickly and evenly spread. No plants had been able to seed themselves in the granite, so – once the ivy was gone – it was quite bare. Tamsin easily found the *M* she was looking for. She recognized it because it was bigger than the other *M* she found – and the *R* and the *T* and the *N* and the *E* . . . They were all there, waiting for her. At least, all except the *I* of *LIVING*, Josiah's surname (or was it an *O*, and *LOVING*?) and the *O* of *LOVING*, on the first line of the inscription (or was it an *I*, and *LIVING*?). Tamsin giggled at the idea of putting 'In living memory' on somebody's grave.

She never did find those last two letters. They must have been there: she just never found them. After all, every single swallow – and every single bird of every other kind – moults every year; but how many feathers do you see lying around? The world ought to be full of feathers, drifting in draughts and swirling in breezes – but it isn't. It's just one of those things.

Tamsin was sad not to have that *I*, though. She'd picked out from her collection the letters of her name, and there was a gap between the *S* and the *N*. She filled the gap with the *I* – *TAMSIN* – and the effect was OK, only not as good as it might have been.

Busy with her letters, Tamsin had quite forgotten Jemima; and that, of course, was the best way to bring Jemima over. Now she came, ambling and dillying and dallying – but nevertheless curious to see what Tamsin was so interested in. Tamsin was pleased she'd come, but couldn't stop timing, according to the rules, until Jemima was actually lying down.

Tamsin arranged a new row of letters, using the *I* from her own name. *EMIMA*. Pity about the *J*. There was only one *J* –

and only ever had been one – in all the eight lines of writing on the gravestone. And that one seemed firm enough to last out the next hundred years. Tamsin had tested it with her fingers, to make sure it didn't just need a bit of help, but she could tell at once that it was nowhere near ready to fall.

She picked up the *E* and held it out to Jemima, gripping it tightly in case Jemima tried to take it from her and eat it. Jemima's soft, soft muzzle reached out and her lips stretched forward, slightly apart, ready to close on the tit-bit being offered. And then, just before the lips touched it, the nostrils caught a whiff of its rank, metallic smell. Jemima snatched her muzzle away and sneezed violently – like somebody blowing a short, sharp raspberry – and then she shook her head so that her ears slapped the sides of her face.

Tamsin laughed at her. "Silly old goat!" But she was glad that Jemima hadn't tried to eat the letter. For all her contrariness and awkwardness, Jemima knew very well what was what.

Just as Jemima lay down with her shoulder leaning up against Tamsin – and Tamsin looked at her watch and saw that Jemima hadn't made such bad time after all – James arrived.

"Tamsin Language from next door," he said.

"Hello, James," said Tamsin.

James caught sight of the little heap of letters and the arrangement that spelt *EM1MA*. "What are those?" he said.

"Letters," said Tamsin.

"And is that a word?"

"Yes." Tamsin was already feeling fed up with him, and she was going to be as unhelpful as she pleased.

James squatted down and studied *EM1MA*. After a while, "It doesn't say James," he said.

"Of course it doesn't," said Tamsin scornfully. "James isn't the only word in the English language, you know."

James still looked at the puzzle. "What *does* it say, then?"

"Emima."

"Is that the English language?"

"Oh, what do you think?" said Tamsin in exasperation. But James wasn't put off.

46

"I think," he said solemnly – and obviously thinking hard –
"I think that 'Emima' is Tamsin for 'Jemima'."

"You what?" said Tamsin. "Oh, never mind. Just shut up:
you're getting on my nerves."

"I get it now," said James, as if he hadn't heard her.
"Mummy says you live in a world of your own. She says
you're a nice girl, but it's like you understand a different language from other people. And now I know you *do* understand a different language!" He was triumphant. "And I
know what it is. It's the Tamsin language! And I know . . ."

"Oh for God's sake, James!" Tamsin was cross and upset.
"Why can't you clear off?"

"Will you teach me the Tamsin language?"

"Look," said Tamsin, scrabbling about in the collection of
letters, "here's an *A* and an *M* and an *E* and an *S*." She set
them out in order for him. "You can have them. I'd give you
a *J* as well, but there isn't one. Still, if you can't have your
name spelt in English, you may as well spell it in – in the
other way. OK?"

Tamsin could see that James was having difficulty in recog-
nizing the four letters without the initial one that he was used
to. She shuffled them along so that they were ranged beneath
EMIMA, then drew with her finger an imaginary *J* at the
beginning of each line.

"Emima – Jemima. Ames – James. See? It's just the J that's
missing from James, same as it's missing from Jemima." She
picked up the *S* of *AMES* and put it in front of the *A*. "There!
SAME!"

James hurriedly put the *S* back in its proper place.

"Right," said Tamsin. "Now you can run along home with
them, can't you?"

James crammed his letters into one hand, and was about
to go, when he suddenly asked, "Where are you going to
keep yours?"

"Oh, I'll probably keep mine here."

"So will I."

"Fine. Leave them here then. Good-bye."

"We can't just leave them." James looked shocked. "We've
got to *hide* them."

47

"Oh, do what you like with them!" He really was the most irritating person Tamsin had ever known. "Why d'you want to hide them anyway? Who's ever going to come here except for us?"

James gave her a look. Then he said, "Mummy comes." He said it as if he hoped that would be the end of the argument. But Tamsin went on.

"And you really think Mummy's going to pinch your letters?"

"No."

"Well then!"

"Just hide them," said James. "Hide them in case someone else comes here, after we've all gone home."

They hid them under pieces of stone that were lying on the ground nearby. Tamsin hid *EM1MA* under the broken-off tip of an angel's wing (you could tell it was that by the carved feathers) and James hid *AMES* under a small, squarish chunk of milky-white marble. The remaining letters they scattered again amongst the granite chips on Ann Maria's grave.

MORE LETTERS

Jessie Lawson was furious. It was Friday afternoon, the summer fair had just arrived in town – and there was a bus strike. All through the diary lesson, Tamsin watched little scraps of paper being passed to and fro between Jess and Greg, who were trying to think of ways of getting to the fair now that the buses were off. Every time Jess wrote or received a note, Tamsin could sneak a glance at what it said.

'Bikes?' said one of Greg's.

Tamsin didn't need to read what Jess wrote back to know what the answer would be. She knew that Mrs Lawson was a bit of a fusspot, and wouldn't allow Jess to cycle into town if she'd be coming out again after dark.

'Hitch?' Greg wrote next.

'Oh yes, Mum would really LOVE that!' Jess wrote. And then she added, 'Moron!' And then, even as she was swivelling round in her chair to pass the note back to Brenda (who would pass it to Steve who would pass it to Greg), just before she slipped it on to Brenda's desk, she added two wildly sprawling kisses.

Tamsin couldn't really be bothered to read the notes after that. There was just one which caught her attention, because it was in a different handwriting. It was addressed to Greg: 'Why don't you all come round mine tonight – for a change – as we can't get into town? Love, Karen.' Greg had forwarded it to Jess with a big question mark and lots of exclamation marks added on. Jess sent it back to Greg with a very rude word scribbled right across the middle.

No one had said anything to Tamsin about the fair or the bus strike. And that was fine, because she wasn't interested in either. She would be baby-sitting as usual, and it made no difference to her whether other people bussed, biked or parachuted into town. She had very little to do with Greg and Jess's lot these days – and they had nothing to do with her.

At the end of the lesson, notes were still zipping back and forth: evidently, there still hadn't been a decision on what to do with the evening. Tamsin left the classroom quickly, as she always did now. By collecting her bike ahead of the others, she avoided the awkwardness of having to walk with them to the gates and then cycle away on her own. Today, she put her stuff in her bag and left so promptly that Jess hadn't even closed her exercise book before she was gone. And as soon as she had gone, one more note landed on Jess's desk.

Jess looked up to see who had dropped it, and almost chucked it disdainfully away when she saw that it was from the Pedaller. But Paul stood his ground and said, "Go on. Read it. If you like the idea, give us a ring." Then he went out, and Jess unfolded the note and began to read.

The note was quite long – it covered a whole side of A4 paper – and Jess was astounded by the information set down in it. It ended with the Pedaller's idea for an evening's entertainment. Jess didn't exactly like the idea, but as all their original plans for the evening had crashed in ruins about their ears . . . Well, anything seemed better than nothing. Besides, it could do no real harm. And anyway, Tamsin was asking for it, wasn't she?

Jess got up and went over to where Greg was still putting things away in his bag. She handed him the note, and as he held it up to read, she saw that the Pedaller had written his telephone number on the back.

As Tamsin cycled back to Whenock, heavy, dark clouds were massing together ahead of her. She pedalled faster and faster: there's nothing worse than being caught in the rain on your bike.

When she reached Great Whenock church, parked her bike as usual and hurried round the side, she half expected that Jemima wouldn't be there – that Mrs Plummer would already have taken her home, to beat the rain.

But Mrs Plummer must have been hoping that the rain wouldn't come, or at least not yet. Jemima was there all right, though she seemed restless and anxious. She kept swinging her head from side to side and then throwing it right round, over her shoulders, so that her nose almost brushed her backbone. It was a funny movement, but Tamsin knew what it meant. It was what Jemima always did when she saw Mrs Plummer coming to take her home for milking and a bucket of food. It meant impatience to be off.

Tamsin didn't play the timing game today. First she looked under the fragment of stone angel's wing, as she had done every day since the day she'd found the letters, to make sure *EM1MA* was still there. Then, instead of choosing a spot to sit down and wait, she went and stood beside Jemima – who was also standing – and rubbed her tassels and ran her fingers along her backbone.

"Don't worry, Mima," she said. "I won't let you get wet." And that was when the first drops fell.

Soon it was pouring. Tamsin spread her arms and hunched her shoulders and bent over Jemima so that her jacket made a kind of roof for her to stand under. It was a thin, summer jacket, but it would have been better than nothing, only Jemima wouldn't stand still. She made little rushes to and fro, all the time tugging at the end of her chain and looking towards the church, hoping to see Mrs Plummer come round the corner. She complained all the time, too, in long, loud, monotonous bleats that only broke off for her to take a breath and start again.

It seemed like years before Mrs Plummer came, though actually it was only minutes. When she did come, she looped a bit of rope through Jemima's collar, unclipped the chain, and they were away. Jemima almost pulled Mrs Plummer over, she set off at such a pace.

It was Tamsin's job to empty out the water bucket and bring it back to the house. Even in the downpour, she didn't forget, and now she dashed after Jemima and Mrs Plummer with the pail clanking at her side. When she reached her bike, leaning against the wall of the church, she hooked the handle of the bucket over one of the handlebars and dashed on again, pushing the bike and clanking more than ever. For a moment, when she turned out of the churchyard gate on to the pavement, and stopped crunching the gravel of the churchyard path beneath her feet, she thought she heard gravel still being crunched, back by the church. But the rain was drumming so hard on the undergrowth that she couldn't be sure; and the yew hedge was now between her and the church, so she couldn't look back. Yes, it was probably the rain: this was the kind of rain that made so much racket you could believe there was a whole army tramping along behind you.

It was dry and warm in Jemima's shed; but Jemima herself was dripping. Mrs Plummer said she'd be fine and that a bit of rain never affected her except to make her grumpy. Tamsin said, couldn't she towel her down all the same, just to be on the safe side? So Mrs Plummer fetched a ragged old towel that she used as a floor cloth, and Tamsin got to work.

But she didn't have time to finish the job. Mrs Plummer had decided to milk Jemima early today, seeing that here she was now, ready and waiting. "I might as well," she said, "and then I won't have to come out in the rain again later on."

Tamsin was learning how to milk. Two weeks back, she'd asked Mrs Plummer whether she could have a go, and Mrs Plummer had shown her how to hold the top of the teat between her thumb and forefinger, and shut it off by squeezing with her thumb; then you had to close tight your second, third and fourth fingers, one after the other, and as you did that, the milk you'd trapped in the teat with your thumb was squeezed out at the bottom. The teat felt firm and round when you first took hold of it – like a smooth, fat carrot – but when you'd finished squeezing, it was shrivelled and floppy. Then you unclasped your hand, and at once more milk came down from the udder, and made the teat full and firm again.

Tamsin could now milk with both hands – one on each teat – but she was still a bit slow. If Mrs Plummer had time to spare, she let Tamsin milk Jemima right through, till no more milk would come; but mostly she took over from her half-way, or even earlier, to get the milking finished quickly. Today, Tamsin was glad to hand over to Mrs Plummer after only a few squeezes. Mrs Plummer had certainly been right about the rain making Jemima grumpy: although she had her usual bucket of goat mix to eat, she shuffled and stamped her feet and occasionally darted her head round to pull Tamsin's hair. Mrs Plummer made threatening, growly noises at Jemima every time she misbehaved: even so, towards the end, when Mrs Plummer herself was milking, Jemima managed to get one of her hind feet into the pail and overturn it completely. When Mrs Plummer had stopped swearing, Tamsin could just hear a sort of slow, hissing sigh, as all the tiny bubbles in the milk froth disintegrated, and the milk seeped down through the straw on the shed floor.

After that, there was only a little more milk to come. Because the inside of the pail was now mucky from Jemima's foot, the last bit of milk looked mucky too, with little specks of dust and dirt floating in it.

"That'll have to go to the cat," said Mrs Plummer crossly. She looked Jemima in the eye. "Ooh, I could strangle you, you old devil!" Tamsin held her breath as she saw Mrs Plummer reach fiercely for Jemima's throat. But she let it out again, seeing the fingers take hold of Jemima's tassels and give them a fierce, fond tug-and-rub. Jemima half-closed her eyes, and burped.

Tamsin said she'd stay in the shed for a bit, to finish the towelling job. She could leave the Plummers' garden by the path round the side of the house. Mrs Plummer looked doubtful. "Never mind Jemima," she said, "*you* must be soaked to the skin."

"I'm not," said Tamsin quickly, though she was. "I had my jacket on, remember."

"Well, don't be too long. Oh, and you can drop the towel inside the porch on your way out." Mrs Plummer put up her anorak hood, drawing the strings so tightly round it that her face became all nose and eyes. She said, "Bye then, love," from a mouth that no longer existed; then she left.

Tamsin set to work on Jemima again. Outside, the rain was falling as hard as ever, but Jemima was calmer now – now that she was under cover, with a bucket of goat mix inside her, and her udder emptied and comfortable. Beyond the open shed door, the rough, hard-baked mud of the enclosure held the rain in little pools, and as more rain fell, it plashed loudly into these. It thrummed, too, on the shed roof, so that Tamsin could hardly hear herself speak when she said anything to Jemima.

And then it happened. Just as it had happened five weeks before, the night that Tamsin had first sat in the shed.

BANG!

And darkness.

And rain plashing and thrumming.

And . . .

No, it wasn't the same as last time. Tamsin froze and listened, and felt Jemima listening too.

Just outside the shut door, above the noise of the rain, there had been a voice. A voice that tried to whisper but ended in a whine.

"Eughhh! I've trod in some goat's doings!"

And then another voice, whispering loudly: "Shuddup! Come on, let's get out of here."

And now that Tamsin was listening, she could make out the sound of feet – a lot of feet – squelching through the sodden enclosure, and away.

Tamsin cried. Not as she might have cried five weeks ago, because one of the Plummers was going to find her in the goat shed in the morning. No, that didn't matter any more – even though they'd fixed the catch on the door now, and would know that it couldn't have been a mere accident. She wasn't crying, either, at the prospect of spending a whole night in the shed – although there was no chance, this time, that James might have heard the door bang, above the noise of the rain outside and the noise, inside, of the TV programme he'd be watching.

Tamsin cried because it had been Jess out there. Karen Halliday had whined about the goat droppings, but it had been Jess who'd told her to shut up.

Tamsin felt so sad and angry and bewildered and . . . and *strange*, that she thought she must burst any minute, or just softly disintegrate and seep down through the straw like the spilt milk of half an hour ago. If only she could! How lovely it

54

would be simply to trickle away without a trace.

Everything was so complicated now. There had been a time when Tamsin would have been out there with the others, ganging up on people and plotting clever schemes. It had been a good time; fun and exciting. Whenock Primary. She and Jess always the leaders. What a joke it had been, pushing Titch Martin into the nature pond – and planting all those unstamped library books on Susie Knight. She could remember so clearly what it had been like to be on the other side that it was as if a part of her – another Tamsin – was still there. What a laugh, shutting someone up in a shed with a goat! Brilliant!

But it was she that was shut in the shed. Tamsin. She wasn't that other Tamsin any more, outside with the gang. She was the Titch, she was the Susie now. And now, more and more, she was beginning to feel what they must have felt. Furious.

And then the shed door opened.

For a moment, Tamsin was dazzled by the sudden light, dulled as it was by rain and the overcast sky. Then she rubbed her eyes and saw who it was who had lifted the latch. It was the Pedaller.

He looked embarrassed, standing there peering in at the goat and the girl. Tamsin and Jemima were staring back without a word. Then he started to speak, quickly and urgently.

"Sorry," he said. "Sorry I brought them to the church-yard. I only meant them to have a look. I thought they'd get bored and go back to Swinston long before you came round here. But then you went and left early." He sounded accusing. "You've *never* left that early before. And they wanted to follow you. I couldn't stop them. And they shut you up in here." He paused, but only *plash plash plash* filled the silence. "Anyway, I thought I'd better let you out when they'd gone."

Perhaps he thought Tamsin might cry some more, and thank him for his kindness. He might even have dreamed that she'd say sorry for all the harm she'd done to him. If he did think that, or, in his wildest dreams, imagine that she'd see things in that way, then he was very wrong.

"Pig!" she said. "You scrawny little runt! You scraggy chicken. D'you think it's clever, or what, to spy on someone? D'you think it's artistic to muck up someone's whole life? Well, I'll tell you what it is: it's *weird*. And *you're* weird. Everyone thinks you're a weirdo – Jess, Greg and everyone. I mean, what would they think about you going and letting me out like this? I mean, that just proves it, doesn't it? There's got to be something wrong with you. I tell you, I pity you. I wouldn't be you for anything!"

"*Me* weird? That's great, coming from *you*!" Paul sounded bitter now. "Silly cow! Can't you see! Can't you see what's been happening?"

But Tamsin wouldn't listen any more. She snatched up Mrs Plummer's towel and rushed out of the shed. As she passed Paul, she deliberately swished the towel over her shoulder so that it slapped him in the face. He caught hold of it and jerked her round.

"Here," he said. "They left this behind. They hung it on the door." He thrust into Tamsin's hand an old, white polystyrene swimming float – the kind that's rounded at one end, like a gravestone. There was a loop of string fixed on, to hang it by.

Tamsin was mystified. Was it some deadly sign for her, like the black spot in *Treasure Island*, or the drowned cat strung up outside someone's bedroom door in a horror film she'd once watched? She shuddered. Then she turned the thing over, to look at the other side – and saw.

In letters that she recognized, their little pegs pressed into the soft polystyrene to hold them in place, a notice had been written:

BABY-SITTING

DO NOT DISTURB

REVENGE

Tamsin's thinking was muddled as she rode through the rain to Swinston, the polystyrene notice board jiggling about in her bicycle basket. She was vaguely aware that something had come to an end, and that perhaps it had come to an end a long time ago, only no one had bothered to say so before now. Anyway, one thing was quite clear: her situation couldn't possibly be worse. Nothing she might do could make anything worse than it was now.

And that was why she was cycling to Swinston. Now that there was no point in pretending any more, she was going to do exactly what she felt like doing. It wasn't fair that Jess and Greg should be able to pry into somebody else's way of life, and laugh, and walk away laughing. They might not think that it mattered, but it did. It did.

Tamsin felt like killing Jess.

When she reached Greg's house, she could hear loud music coming from the loft above the garage, and there were half a dozen bikes flung down just inside the open garage door. So, they'd come straight back here from Whenock, as Tamsin had been hoping. Good. She leaned her own bike against the fence at the edge of the short driveway. Usually, she was careful to leave her bike under cover when it was raining, but today she didn't. In any case, she'd be on it again so soon that the saddle would hardly have time to get wet.

Tamsin quietly went into the garage. Up above, the music pounded on. She picked her way through all the bikes, and edged along between the wall and the side of Greg's parents' car. At the far end of the garage was the trap-door up into the loft. It was open, and the aluminium ladder was in place.

There were two square hooks at the top of the ladder, which fitted into two iron staples driven into the side of the wooden frame of the hatchway.

Cautiously, Tamsin stepped to the foot of the ladder and looked up. Only the rafters looked back at her through the hatch. Good. That meant that everyone was up at the other end of the loft – the end over the garage door. Yes, she could just hear them, through the din of the radio. They seemed to be playing cards, and laughing a lot. They'd have all the cushions and the packs of cards and the radio up at that end, too: no reason, then, for anyone to come over to the hatchway and disturb Tamsin in her work.

She took hold of the ladder with both hands, one on each side. Anyone watching her would have thought she was about to climb up. But she kept her feet planted firmly on the floor – slightly apart, because she was preparing to brace herself. Carefully, carefully, she tried to force the ladder upwards, so that the hooks at the top would rise out of the staples that held them. The hooks did begin to rise, but much more suddenly than Tamsin had expected – and with a loud squawk of metal grating on metal.

Tamsin stiffened, feeling sick. She waited for the inevitable face to appear in the hatchway above her. But nobody came. She listened for the sound of people jumping to their feet, but heard only the radio and the sounds of continued card-playing. And then she heard another squawk, very like the one she'd just made herself. It was amazing. It was – the radio!

The radio in the loft, Tamsin remembered, had always been on the way out, and now, it seemed, had finally cracked. Too much 'top vol thrashing', as Greg used to call it. Anyway, the radio was now turning drum rolls into machine-gun fire, cymbal clashes into rashers of bacon being thrown into enormous, spitting frying pans; and electric guitar chords came out as – well – as the sound made by someone unhooking a giant aluminium ladder from a pair of giant iron staples. *PUM-PUM-PUM-PUM-PUM-PUM-PUM PUM-PUM SIZZZZLE SQUAWK*!

Tamsin waited for the next burst of gunfire, then the sizzling oil, and then, with all her might, she hoisted the ladder upwards again. *SQUAAAAWK*! The hooks, which had before risen only a little way out of their holders, now rose out clear, and Tamsin swayed drunkenly for a moment, with the ladder swaying above her. Then she steadied herself and placed the ladder's feet back on the garage floor. She steered the aluminium hooks back to the frame of the hatchway, and brought them to rest against it, each one just slightly to one side of the staple that had held it before.

The ladder looked just the same as before – same angle, same everything – only now, ten feet up from the hard concrete floor, it was no longer hooked to the frame of the hatchway. It was just propped there. Tamsin turned to go.

And as she turned, she caught sight of a pair of roller skates hanging from a nail in the wall. She took the skates down, and stood still, thinking. There were some bricks stacked up against the wall, and she took two of them as well. She put the skates and the bricks on the floor near the ladder.

She knelt down and, with one hand, took hold of the bottom rung of the ladder. She eased its feet up off the floor – up and out, so that the top stayed where it was, pinned like the hand of a clock to the centre of the clock face. With her free hand, she steered one of the skates into the space underneath one foot of the ladder, and then the other skate under the other foot. Her arm was trembling with the effort of supporting the ladder, but now she could lower it once more. Each foot came to rest on its own little wheeled platform.

Tamsin shunted a brick up against the front of each skate – and the bricks were just heavy enough to stop the skates rolling forward. Any more weight on the ladder – just one foot placed on the top rung – and the skates would shoot away, pushing the bricks in front of them like empty Black Magic boxes before a road-sweeper's broom.

The whole thing reminded Tamsin of one of those crazy contraptions in the comics that she used to read. In a comic, Hannah Planner (or perhaps Dora Jar) would have stepped on the ladder and ended up – *WHAM*! *BAM*! *SPLAT*! – sitting on the floor with her eyes going round like spinning tops, and stars and squiggly lines coming out from her head.

Then, when you turned the page, she'd be up and running again as if nothing had happened.

It was funny to think that comics had always seemed like another world, that you could leap into to escape the real one for an hour or an afternoon. Now comics were a part of the real world – but that was far away. Tamsin was in a strange, new one, and there was no going back.

"Jessie!" she called. "Jess-ie!" But she might as well have been standing on another planet, calling across the universe: with the noise of the radio, nobody heard her.

She moved over to the light switch – the one that controlled the light in the loft. They had the light on up there at the moment. Tamsin flipped the switch up, then down again; up, then down again.

Somebody turned the radio off, and Tamsin heard Karen say, "Ooh, it's creepy." Somebody else said, "Shhh!"

Then Tamsin called again, "Jess-ie!" and switched the light off one last time.

There was a noise of confused shouting and people scrambling to their feet at the other end of the loft. Tamsin raced to the garage door, jumped over one of the bikes, tripped over another, recovered herself and raced on. As she mounted her own bike, there was a terrible crash and a scream, behind her, in the garage.

Tamsin shot out of the driveway and into the road.

"Please let her not be hurt! Oh, please let her not be dead!" But there was no going back.

Head down; hands, with knuckles white, gripping handlebars; feet pumping round and round.

The rain was a comfort to her now. It drenched her, as she pedalled frantically back to Whenock, just as it drenched the trees and the hedgerows and the grass and the earth. However weird and different she was, she was still normal enough to get wet in the rain.

It felt as though an age had passed since Tamsin had last been in Great Whenock churchyard: she could hardly believe that she'd been there only a couple of hours before. Everything had still been all right then.

After she'd leaned her bike up against the church wall, she

took the piece of polystyrene out of the basket and made her way towards the far end of the churchyard. It looked sad and desolate there now, with the rain coming down and no Jemima. She went straight to Ann Maria's grave. But when she reached it, she hardly recognized it: all but a few of the letters had been prized from the face of the stone. They lay on the ground round about, twisted and broken.

Tamsin swore out loud. She hadn't imagined any damage beyond the theft of the particular letters that she'd come here to put back – the ones that had been pegged into the polystyrene. She hadn't imagined the kind of damage that's done purely for its own sake.

"You vandals!" she shouted.

She crouched down on the grave and scrabbled with her hands, like a dog about to bury a bone. The rain continued. She scooped out a little trench in the granite chips, and went on scooping, right down into the earth underneath. She stopped only when the earth became too hard-packed for her fingers to scrape up.

In her trench, Tamsin laid all the poor letters that had been pulled off the gravestone. She gathered them up as best she could, and tried to straighten out the bent ones, untwist the ones that had got twisted. Because the metal was so soft, some of them tore in two when she tried to put right their distorted shapes; others were already in pieces.

The whole and the mutilated, the straight and the twisted: Tamsin laid them all in the little grave. She put with them the letters that she now picked out of the piece of polystyrene. Letter by letter, the hateful message disappeared, and when Tamsin had finished, the polystyrene was blank except for the U and the hyphen, which had been inked in with a black felt-tip pen. By themselves, these looked ugly and ridiculous: the dustbin, Tamsin thought to herself, was the best place for *them*.

When all the letters she could find had been gathered up, there was nothing left to do but cover them over. First she put back the earth, then the granite. In the process, some of the earth got smeared on to some of the granite, making it look grimy – but the rain would soon wash it clean again.

Soon, no one would ever guess that the patch had been disturbed at all.

Tamsin stood up. The only letters that remained unburied were the few that were still in place on the stone. Or so it seemed. Tamsin brought one hand close up to her face, fingers folded over palm. She opened her fingers – and there was the *J*.

A week ago, Tamsin would have jumped for joy to have the *J* in her hand. Now it seemed sad. The *J* was just another part of the ruins.

But it was a bit more than that, too – which was why Tamsin hadn't been able to make herself bury it along with the other letters. Now she carried it over to the spot where the piece of angel's wing was. She picked up the clump of stone feathers and found *EM1MA*, safe and sound, underneath. She added the *J*, gently replaced the stone, and headed back to her bike.

When Tamsin got home, her mother was out. It was only half past six, but Mr Langridge made her get into a hot bath straight away, and then put on some pyjamas that were warm from the airing cupboard. He kept asking her what she'd been doing to get so very wet, and Tamsin said, "Oh, cycling around." She didn't say *why* she'd been cycling around. Well, she couldn't, could she? She couldn't say she'd been killing Jess.

DISASTER

Tamsin caught a bad cold from her soaking on Friday, and had to stay indoors all weekend. If she'd been in a book or a film, she thought wistfully, it would have been pneumonia and she'd have been close to death. As it was, the cold wasn't even serious enough for them to get the doctor round.

Every time the phone rang, Tamsin was sure it was going to be Jessie's parents; and whenever someone came to the door, she imagined it was the police. Would they take her away even when she was ill? Probably. They'd ask exactly how ill she was, and find out that she wasn't ill enough to see a doctor, and then they'd bundle her into their van.

When Tamsin slept, she dreamed that she was pushing Jess over the edge of a cliff, or off a railway bridge, or from the top of the Eiffel Tower (when they climbed up it one day on their class trip to Paris). Whatever Jess was pushed off, she always screamed that scream as she fell.

When Mr Langridge went to the shops in Whenock High Street on Saturday morning, he bought Tamsin a comic. It was the one that had always been her favourite, but it seemed boring and silly now. The only thing that could have taken her mind off things was Jemima.

Tamsin hoped that the Pedaller had shut the gate properly when he left Jemima's enclosure on Friday. She should have gone round there to check, before she'd finally come home that evening. Still, Mrs Plummer would have called round if there were something wrong, because as far as she knew, Tamsin was the last person in the goat enclosure that day.

Tamsin wished she could sit with Jemima now: after Friday's downpour, it was fine and warm again, and Jemima would be back in the churchyard, browsing and dozing and chewing the cud. You could never shock Jemima, and Tamsin longed to go to her and whisper what she'd done. But she wasn't allowed outdoors till Monday – and that, of course, was to go to school.

Tamsin had got into the habit of cycling to school early, so that she didn't have to go with Jess. Today, too, she set off early, just as if it were the same as any other day. When she arrived, and went to her locker to get out some books, she couldn't help having a peep into Jessie's locker – just to see whether somebody had already cleared it out. Nobody had, yet. Tamsin went to her place and sat down. She was the only one in the classroom. She folded her arms on her desk, and rested her head on them, face down, wondering what was going to happen to her.

When Rebecca Trisk and Evie Kelman had been caught stealing sweets from the newsagent, they'd had to go and see the Head, Mrs White, and afterwards they'd come out crying. But when Robert Newton's sister was killed in a car accident, Mr Lively had sent him to lovely Miss Mayhew, the maths teacher, and Miss Mayhew had had to tell him the news. In breaktime, Tamsin and Jess had waited at the far end of the corridor to see what would happen when Robert came out.

The door had opened at last, and there he was – all red in the face and puffy round the eyes, with a bunch of white paper handkerchiefs clutched in one hand. Miss Mayhew stood behind him. He'd taken a couple of steps forward, and then his face had crumpled, like a flower on one of those nature programmes when they show it opening and then, for a special effect, they show that bit in reverse. Robert's face was like the flower closing up, very fast. He turned round and sort of butted his head into Miss Mayhew's skirt, and his paper handkerchiefs floated to the floor like a flock of white doves landing, and Miss Mayhew bent down and hugged him and kissed him.

No wonder people said Mr Lively fancied Miss Mayhew and was going to ask her to marry him. Tamsin wanted to butt *her* head into Miss Mayhew's skirt, and cling to her and be hugged and kissed by her. But she knew it would be Mrs White that she'd have to see. It was all so unfair. Why couldn't people just leave her alone? It was when they wouldn't leave her alone that things went wrong.

The classroom was gradually beginning to fill up. Tamsin could hear the first arrivals coming in, though she didn't bother to lift her head to see who they were. Locker doors banged, chair legs scraped and conversations started up. When it sounded as though the room must be full, a chair scraped very close to Tamsin. Next to her. Someone thumped some books down *on the next-door desk*. Someone *sat down* next to her. Tamsin lifted her head and looked. It was Jess.

Tamsin was so happy that she wanted to say something quite normal, like, 'Had a good weekend?' or, 'Hello!' She knew she wasn't supposed to say things like that any more, but she couldn't help herself.

"Hello," she said. And smiled.

Jess looked at her coldly. "You're *so stupid*," she said. "That was such a *stupid* thing to do on Friday. You could have killed me, you know."

Tamsin knew.

"If it hadn't been for the roller skates, you *would* have killed me. I'd have got right on to the ladder before it gave way, and I'd have fallen. As it was, it was bad enough. Whacked down on the edge of the hatch on my chest: winded myself. Well, I hope you're pleased."

Tamsin was pleased. She hadn't felt this pleased for ages. She thought back to the moment when she'd caught sight of the roller skates on the garage wall, and taken them down. She'd wanted to kill Jess, certainly, and had thought the skates would make her contraption all the more deadly. Perhaps she *was* stupid, as Jess said. But who cared?

"I put the skates there to make it safe," she said.

"Well, next time oil the wheels, why don't you? Safe! D'you know what it's like, being winded? I was thrashing about, with my legs hanging down through the hole, and I would have gone after them if Greg and John hadn't got hold of my arms. *Safe*! God, you're stupid, Tamsin Langridge. You and your stupid goat!"

Tamsin would have taken almost anything from Jess right now, but not that. That wasn't fair. Jemima was good and intelligent – far more intelligent than her or Jess or Greg or anybody else she knew. She wasn't going to stand for Jemima being dragged into this.

"She's not stupid," she said.

"Who isn't?" said Jess. "Oh. Yes it is."

"The goat. She's not stupid."

"It is," said Jess. "It is, because all goats are stupid. I know. My dad went to London Zoo with the bowls, and he said the goats were eating lighted cigarettes. Can't get much more stupid than that, can you?"

"That's rubbish," said Tamsin. "A goat would never do that. Not even if it was starving."

Mr Lively hurried into the classroom with the register under his arm. He sat down, called for silence, and began going through the list of names.

But Jess couldn't let Tamsin have the last word.

"Anyway, how d'you know your precious goat wouldn't eat a lighted cigarette," she whispered, "when you've never even offered it one?"

"How d'you know I haven't?" Tamsin whispered back.

"Give us a break!"

"All right then, I will offer her one. I'll do it after school today – and then you'll see."

Mr Lively came to Tamsin's name on the register. He looked at her hard, with his eyebrows raised. She fell silent, then said, "Yes, sir." Jessie's name was next, and she got the same treatment. "Yes, sir." Then it was "Danny McLintock" – "Yes" – and "Robert Newton" – "Yes, sir" – and as the names went on, Jess got in one more whisper, so quiet and quick that Tamsin only just heard: "You're on. After school in the churchyard. We'll be there."

Throughout the day, Tamsin didn't give much thought to what might happen later on. After her weekend of horrible imaginings and nightmares, the thing that her attention kept straying to, again and again, was Jess: Jess ignoring her in lessons, Jess pushing past her in the dinner queue, but Jess there and normal and alive and well.

Not until Tamsin arrived in the churchyard that afternoon, did she look ahead and wonder. Well, maybe no one would turn up: Jess hadn't said anything more to her since morning registration. And even if they did come, there wouldn't be any cigarettes, so they'd all have to go home again. It wasn't that Tamsin didn't have faith in Jemima, but it seemed mean to put her to the test like that; it would make it *look* as if Tamsin wasn't sure of her.

Jemima was lying in her favourite spot, on top of the table tomb, and Tamsin was sitting beside her, legs dangling over the edge. She hadn't felt like doing the timing test today: she'd gone off the idea of testing altogether. The gritty grey stone of the tomb-top felt warm from the sun, and the sun was warm, too, on Jemima's shining coat. Tamsin stroked and rubbed the rich brown fur, ruffling it into little rivulets by dragging her fingers through it the wrong way – and then smoothing it out by running them back again. Jemima chewed and chewed and occasionally burped.

And then Tamsin saw them coming. Jess and Greg; Karen, Neil, Karl and John. She jumped down from the tomb and stood with her back up against it, waiting. Jemima stayed as she was, only she pricked her ears forward, watching with interest as the six approached.

Jess and Greg came first, with the other four straggling along behind. Tamsin saw that Greg had his arm round Jess.

When they reached Tamsin, Greg said, "Well fancy meeting you here!" and they all laughed – all except Tamsin. She said, "Sorry. We can't do it today. I forgot to bring a cigarette." They laughed again.

Jessie was wearing a denim jacket, and now she fished about in the top pocket and brought out a packet of cigarettes. When she tipped back the top of the packet, Tamsin saw that it was about half-full. Jess gave her wrist a little flick, holding the packet on a level, and four or five cigarettes were shaken forward so that they poked out of the end. They were meant to look inviting, but they reminded Tamsin of blunt gunbarrels – the sort that are mounted on army tanks. Jess turned her back on Tamsin and offered the cigarettes round.

67

Each of the group took one, except for Karl, who had his own. Then Jess swivelled about again, held out her arm, and pointed the last projecting cigarette at Tamsin.

"Fag?" she said.

Tamsin had to stop herself cowering back, as if Jess really were training a gun on her. She managed to stand firm, and shook her head.

"No thanks," she said. "Don't smoke."

"But *you* do, don't you?" Jess looked past Tamsin to Jemima. "Hey, you up there! Want a fag?" She jabbed the packet, with the single cigarette still sticking out from it, in Jemima's direction. Jemima stretched out her neck and parted her lips to take what Jess offered. But Jess was standing too far away. Jemima got to her feet, came to the very edge of the tomb-top, and stretched out again, over Tamsin's shoulder. Jess took two steps forward and moved the cigarette packet towards the space above Tamsin's shoulder, where Jemima's mouth now was.

"No!" Tamsin suddenly flung up her arm, hitting Jemima under the chin and knocking the cigarette out of Jessie's packet. "That's not what you said! You said a *lighted* cigarette."

Jemima sneezed loudly and huffily. She retreated a few steps, shaking her head and waggling her ears.

"Oh, so you admit it eats them unlit, do you?" Jess sneered. "That shows it's *pretty* stupid, for a start."

"Maybe she would," said Tamsin. "Maybe not. But if she does, then that's not because she's stupid. It's because tobacco is a plant. You know, leaves. Like grass."

Behind Jess, Greg sniggered. "And what would you know about grass, Tamsin 'No-Thanks-Don't-Smoke' Langridge?" Behind Greg, the snigger echoed round the other four.

Tamsin ignored Greg, and bent down to pick up the cigarette on the ground at her feet. She looked Jess in the eye. "Lighted," she said.

"OK, OK, keep your hair on!" Jess had taken out one more cigarette from the packet, and put it in her mouth. When she spoke, the cigarette didn't bob up and down like old Mr Haines's did, when he was chatting to someone over

68

his front gate: Jess tightened her lips so that the cigarette stuck out stiff as a nail in a wall. Her voice sounded tight, too, and her whole face somehow seemed to have tightened, hardened. She didn't look like herself any more, Tamsin thought.

Jess slipped the cigarette packet back where it had come from, and brought out an orange plastic lighter from the same place. "Right then," she said. "Who wants a light back there?"

Some of them lit up from Jess, some from Karl. Tamsin felt awkward and embarrassed while she waited for them to finish. The cigarette in her hand was embarrassing. She didn't know how to hold it: that is, she knew how she should hold it if she were going to smoke it, but she couldn't decide how to hold it, seeing that she wasn't. In the end, she let it lie across the four curled-up fingers of her left hand, as if it were the handle of a plastic carrier bag that she was holding by her side.

· Jess turned back to face her, lighting her own cigarette as she did so. She cupped one hand around the little flame at the top of the lighter, while with her lips she held the end of her cigarette in it. She sucked her cheeks in, to draw the flame, and her face looked not only tight and hard, but also suddenly old. Frightening. If only she could see herself, Tamsin thought. And then the cigarette was alight and Jess was holding it between her fingers and smoke was coming out of her nostrils like the jets of steam that mad bulls breathe, in cartoon strips, as they snort and paw the ground, ready to charge.

"OK," said Jess, "now we're all set to enjoy the show. You'd better give it yours –" she glanced at the cigarette Tamsin had picked up "– because I'm not having my hand bitten off by a gormless great goat. Here." She held out the lighter. "Lighting-up time."

Tamsin imagined what it would be like to put the cigarette in her mouth and tighten her lips and cup her hands around the lighter flame. She imagined sucking in her cheeks like an old, old woman.

"No," she said. "I'll take yours and you have this one." So

they swapped, and Jess lit up for a second time, and Tamsin held a burning cigarette in her hand.

"Get up on stage!" somebody shouted. "Go on. Get up there with the goat! Give us an act!"

Tamsin clambered up the rough heap of masonry that Jemima herself always used for getting on and off the top of the tomb. She was soon on a level with Jemima, the cigarette still smouldering safely in her hand. A little breeze gusted some of the smoke across the tomb, fanning it out and letting it hang for a moment like a ghostly tablecloth, raised up from its stone table. Jemima sniffed, widened her nostrils and then sneezed in one of her biggest, most disgusted raspberries ever.

And Tamsin knew then that she had nothing to worry about up there. She knew that Jemima would never go near the lighted cigarette, let alone touch it – let alone *eat* it. Because, in all things, Jemima knew what was what. And Tamsin was so relieved that suddenly she felt she didn't care about anything except this. She looked down and saw six unfriendly faces staring back at her, but they didn't matter now that she was up here and everything up here was going to be all right. She saw Greg with his arm draped round Jessie's shoulders: well, let them, if that was what they wanted. She even saw the beginning of the summer holidays next week and herself with no one to talk to and no one to do things with – but that was the future, and had better take care of itself.

"Give it the fag, then!" someone shouted, and Tamsin moved towards Jemima with the cigarette held out in front of her. Jemima backed away as far as she could, and then stood, with her head held high, her neck straight and her nostrils flared. Tamsin could hear her breathing drily and heavily.

"Look!" She smiled down at the six on the ground. "Can't you see she's scared?"

"You're not trying," said Jess. "You're not giving it a chance. Try again – harder."

Tamsin shuffled forward again with the cigarette, clicking her tongue as she'd heard people clicking at horses to coax them into doing something. Jemima couldn't go back any further, or she'd have fallen over the edge – and she couldn't escape down the heap of rubble because Tamsin blocked the way to that end. She just stood there, rigid. She opened her mouth a little, as if she wanted to pant like a dog, and her eyes were wide.

"There! She's scared, see! She's terrified!" Tamsin was triumphant.

But the others were furious. "It just doesn't know what's good for it," said Jess. "It hasn't learnt yet."

"That's right," said Karl. "It wants teaching." He lumbered round to Jemima's end of the tomb, the others following him. He got close up behind Jemima. His eyes were on a level with the underside of her belly; his thoughts were on a level with the nastiest, meanest things in the world. He raised his hand towards Jemima and touched her – jabbed her belly – with the burning tip of his cigarette.

Mrs Plummer probably didn't hear Jemima's grunt of pain and surprise. What she did hear, as she came round the corner of the church, was the cheering and laughter that drowned it out. What she saw was a group of kids clustered round one end of the old sarcophagus; and Jemima in their midst, perched on top of it; and Tamsin, like a priest, standing over her.

"STOP!" screamed Mrs Plummer.

As she ran forward, seven children scattered. And when she reached the sarcophagus – which had always reminded her of some ancient stone altar – she and Jemima and the gravestones were alone.

That evening, Mrs Plummer knocked on the Langridges' front door. She wouldn't come in, but spoke to Mrs Langridge on the doorstep. She said that she never wanted to see Tamsin anywhere near Jemima again.

OLD HAUNTS

Tamsin thought that life must be about to end. It had been getting steadily worse and worse, and now, like the smooth curves they had to plot on graphs in their maths books, it had levelled out. There was no point in going on with it any further.

She had locked herself in the bathroom and was lying flat on the lino, sobbing. People slashed their wrists in the bath, didn't they? Tamsin had come to the bathroom because it was the only room in the house with a lock on the door – but maybe there were other advantages in it, too. There was the bath, there were her father's razor blades . . .

But why *did* people cut their wrists in the bath? Was it so that there wouldn't be so much mess for their families to clean up afterwards? Or was it because the bathroom was the only room they could lock themselves into and get going without being disturbed?

"Tamsin!" It was her father, rattling the door handle. "Come on, Tamsie. I want to clean my teeth."

"Go away!" she said.

"Tamsin, I want to clean my teeth NOW!"

"Well, *go away* then. I'm only coming out when you're not there!"

She heard him breathe an exaggerated sigh and then stomp off down the stairs. She got up from the floor, unlocked the door and made a dash for her bedroom.

Sitting on her bed, Tamsin thought again. If life wasn't going to end just yet, she must do something to make it bearable. And it was no good trying to explain things to people, either: she'd tried that tonight, with her parents, but they hadn't been able to understand what she was saying. They'd sat her down, when Mrs Plummer had gone, and asked her, "What's been going on then? What's all this about Jemima?" And Tamsin had begun at the beginning, with Swinston and Jess and Greg and Greg's loft and the Pedaller – and her parents had stopped her before she'd got even one tenth of the way through, and asked, "But what's any of this got to do with what Mrs Plummer was talking about?" And Tamsin had lost her temper and shouted, "It's not just Jemima, you know!"

In the end, her parents had given up, and said they'd need to hear everybody's side of the story before they could sort it out: they were going to arrange a meeting with Tamsin, Mrs Plummer, Mr Lively, Jessie, Greg, Paul – even their parents, if they wanted to come. Tamsin had made up her mind on the spot about one thing: *she* certainly wasn't going to be around to be mucked about and meddled with any more.

Sitting on her bed, Tamsin knew what she had to do. She'd run away – tonight – and she'd take Jemima with her.

Mr and Mrs Langridge took ages to get to bed. Tamsin almost fell asleep once or twice, waiting for them to settle, even though she had her jeans on under the bedclothes, and felt so nervous and excited. When she could hear no more movement, she crept to her bedroom door and opened it – only to see a thin line of light under her parents' door. She had to wait an age for them to turn the light off, and then another, to give them time to fall asleep. After that, she felt it was safe to tip-toe downstairs.

In the kitchen, she took a pale blue china cup from the cupboard and clipped its handle to the key-ring hanging from one of her belt hooks. The cup was to milk Jemima into. Mostly, Tamsin would drink the milk herself (babies lived on just milk, didn't they?) but when she needed to buy clothes or something, she could sell some of it at the roadside. She'd sell it in bottles that she'd take from people's doorsteps, early in the morning, before the milkman came. Cars full of holiday-makers from London would stop and buy pints and pints. Little children would get out and stroke

Jemima, while their parents paid Tamsin lots of money for all the bottles of good, fresh goats' milk they'd packed away in their boot.

Next Tamsin went to the dirty linen basket, over by the washing machine. She rummaged through all the sheets and towels and clothes that had been put there for the wash, until she found her mother's dressing-gown. It still had its cord with it, threaded through the special loops. Tamsin pulled the cord out and stuffed it into her pocket. That was to tie on to Jemima's collar, and lead her by. They would wander together through the open countryside, where the grass verges were wide and lush. Jemima would eat as they went along, and drink at whatever streams they came to. They would dilly-dally down leafy lanes and linger in buttercup meadows, and wherever they went, the sun, shining through the trees, would cast dappled shade, like lace, over their path.

Tears welled up in Tamsin's eyes as she pictured to herself what was to come. She hurried from the kitchen, and out through the front door.

The moon was almost full tonight. It made Tamsin think of that other night, weeks ago, when the moon had been full and she had made her way, as she was doing now, down to the end of the Plummers' garden. Then, she had wanted just an hour with Jemima; now, since she'd been forbidden to be with her for even one minute, she was going to take her away to be alone with her forever.

She let herself into the goat enclosure and went over to the open doorway of the shed. There, glimmering through the thick, black darkness inside, were the two white stripes, over in the far corner, that Tamsin had worked out last time were the white markings on Jemima's face.

"Mima!" she said softly. "Mima! Hello!"

In answer, there was a violent rustling of straw as Jemima got to her feet and was all of a sudden hurtling towards Tamsin. It flashed through Tamsin's mind that perhaps this was the old dream coming true: Jemima running towards her when Tamsin called her name. But Jemima ran past Tamsin, brushing Tamsin's jeans as she pelted out through the doorway; she stopped only when she reached the opposite side of

74

the enclosure, brought to a standstill by the fence.

Tamsin was puzzled. She could only think that the full moon had affected Jemima's brain: people said that a full moon sometimes made animals act funny. She approached again, holding out her hand coaxingly.

"Mima, Mima! Come on, Jemima, it's only me!"

But Jemima scurried away again, and Tamsin could see, when she stopped and turned, that her eyes were wide, her nostrils flared and her feet splayed apart, ready for another dash.

It's only me. Tamsin thought about that. Me, who waved in your face a glowing, smouldering point of fire. Me, who smiled when you were scared. Me, who trapped you on a high stone platform. Me who caused you to be burnt with a lighted cigarette. Oh yes, thought Tamsin, you're right to be afraid and I'd be ashamed of you if you weren't. You'd be stupid if you weren't afraid of *me*!

Tamsin knew the time had come to give up, and she did. Yet she couldn't bring herself to go home. She left the goat enclosure and the Plummers' garden, and collected her bike from next door. Dimly she remembered a place that once she had looked on from a long way off, wishing to be quiet and alone. Where had she been that she'd so badly needed to escape? And then she remembered: Greg's loft. It had been through the loft window that she'd seen the far-away tree, and imagined herself sitting underneath it. On the day of the dead hen and the nicknaming of the Pedaller.

Tamsin cycled to Swinston – and through it, out into the farmland on the other side. Once she was over the level crossing, she had to guess which hedgerow would lead to her particular tree – and she certainly wasn't going to be able to recognize the tree itself. But then, she supposed, any tree would do.

In the end, she laid down her bike at the side of the road where a wheat field met up with a potato field. The two were divided by a straggly hedge that Tamsin now followed, to get to a tree she'd spotted some way along it. The farmer had sown both crops as near to the edges of the fields as he could get, and though Tamsin tried to keep to the top of the little ridge that the hedge grew on, she sometimes tripped over a clod of earth and stumbled down into the wheat. When that happened, she left behind her a small bay of flattened stems that put a curve in the straight line of the edge of the crop. Other times, she fell through a gap in the hedge into the dark green, bushy potato plants on the other side.

The tree, when she reached it, turned out to be old and gnarled and half-dead: the branches on one side had grown leaves, but the others were bare and looked dry and brittle. There was practically nowhere to sit, but Tamsin eventually found a space just big enough, between two roots. She crouched down between the roots, with her knees drawn up to her chest and her arms clasped round them. She was extremely uncomfortable.

It was amazing, thought Tamsin, how cold a summer's night could be. You'd never imagine that a day as fine as today had been would turn into a night as cold as this. And damp, too. Tamsin could feel the damp of the earth beneath her, through the seat of her jeans. She closed her eyes and tried to sleep. Perhaps she'd die in her sleep, from the cold and the damp, and they'd find her here in the morning and be sorry.

But Tamsin didn't die. She didn't even sleep. Both her legs went to sleep, completely, and that was all. When she could bear the cold no longer, she got up, - but at once collapsed because it felt as though her legs weren't there any more. For a while, she writhed about among the potato plants, pulling faces and moaning, as pins and needles set in and, excruciatingly slowly, feeling crept back. Then she got up, hobbled to her bike and cycled away.

Tamsin cycled back to Great Whenock. It was still dark. She cycled right through the village, and into Little Whenock. That was where the primary school was: next to Little Whenock church.

Tamsin hadn't been back there since she'd left, last July. At least, she'd often been back when she'd dreamed up tiny, keyhole pictures inside those 'o's in textbooks at Swinston – but she'd never been back like this. Now, as she wheeled her bike through the gates, she knew that she didn't belong any more

– and the school didn't belong to her now, either. It belonged to the children who'd been in the classes under hers, and it belonged for the first time to the newest Infants who hadn't been coming to school last year at all. The school was theirs now. It wasn't hers.

She left her bike leaning against the low wall around the Infants' sandpit, and wandered over the grass to the climbing-frame. She sat on a bar, swinging her legs and feeling like a trespasser in another world. The climbing-frame – which, before, had dared her to hang from terrifying heights and swing across impossible gaps – now seemed small. If she stood on tip-toe, she could touch the top bar without leaving the ground.

But she didn't go away just yet. Partly, it was nice, in a sad sort of way, to think about how she and Jess had used to play here; partly, it was good to feel her own strangeness here now – to breathe it deep into her lungs, so that she'd never again make the mistake of thinking she could ever come back.

It was getting light. Birds were beginning to sing. Tamsin wasn't wearing a watch, but she thought it must soon be time for school to start. What would happen if little children coming through the gates of Whenock Primary caught sight of a great, tall girl sitting swinging her legs on their climbing-frame? They'd stare and point and wonder what she was doing there. Hurriedly, Tamsin slid off the bar and went to pick up her bike.

Back at home, all was quiet. Tamsin nearly forgot to replace the blue china cup and her mother's dressing-gown cord, and had to turn round half-way up the stairs. The clock in the kitchen told her it was only quarter past four.

Even with so little sleep, Tamsin woke at quarter to eight as usual. Before she set off for school, her mother handed her a note to take to Mr Lively. It was about organizing that meeting, she said.

"And mind you give it to him, Tamsin! It needs a written reply, so I'll know if you haven't."

Tamsin put the note in her bag, and the bag in her bicycle basket, but she didn't cycle to school – not straight away. She went round first to Great Whenock churchyard, where there was something that she urgently needed to do. Really, she should have done it last night, instead of roaming all over the countryside on her bike. But then, going to those places last night had been something that needed to be done, too.

Tamsin was glad to find that Jemima wasn't yet in the churchyard. She made her way quickly over to her piece of angel's wing, and lifted it off its treasure.

EM1MA. Five letters. There were only five letters there.

At first, Tamsin was taken aback, but she instantly recovered – and reasoned. Of course, it was James. "Selfish brat!" she muttered as she moved over to his chunk of marble. She kicked it aside, and found underneath a woodlouse and a pale pink centipede. Nothing else. The woodlouse rolled itself up into a ball; the centipede scuttled away.

Up until now, Tamsin had been quite calm: she had decided what she was going to do, and although she wouldn't exactly enjoy it, there would be some satisfaction in doing it properly. It would be like coming to the end of a page in one of her exercise books, and blowing on the ink – she'd learnt to do that now, instead of stroking it – before she turned over and began writing on a fresh, new page.

But now she wouldn't be able to do the thing properly. She'd be turning over the page without the ink having fully dried.

"Blast you, James!" shouted Tamsin out loud, and burst into tears. It seemed to her that she'd cried more in the last week than she'd cried in the whole of the rest of her life. Tears seemed always to be ready and waiting now, to come whenever the next thing should go wrong.

She went back to *EM1MA* and picked the letters up. She'd just have to go ahead with her plan, even though she hadn't got the *J*. It wouldn't be as good without the *J*, but it would have to do. With the letters in her hand, she went over and stood on Ann Maria's grave.

"Tamsin Language."

Tamsin hadn't heard James coming. He'd come up behind her, and now stared with interest at her red, puffy eyes and wet cheeks.

"You look all funny," he said. "You've been crying."

"Yes. Because of you, you nasty little thief! You've mucked everything up. You stole the *J*!"

"*You* stole it," said James. "*You* took it off the gravestone."

"I didn't: someone else did. I found it on the ground. Anyway, you can give it back now."

"I never stole it!" James stamped his foot.

"OK, OK. Neither of us stole it. I found it, you borrowed it. Now, finders keepers – so you'd better give it back to me."

James dug deep into his trouser pocket and brought out all the letters of his name. He handed Tamsin the *J*. Then he looked at the *A* and the *M* and the *E* and the *S*.

"They won't be lucky any more," he said gloomily. "That one made them lucky. I took it to school to keep Kerry Walsh away – and she never came near me. But now she'll bash my face in. I know she will. She keeps saying she's going to bash my face in, and now I haven't got a lucky charm to keep her off."

He looked as though he might be about to cry. Tamsin felt she ought to comfort him: that seemed only fair.

"Don't worry," she said. "It's nearly the end of term. And after the holidays, Kerry Walsh will have forgotten all about it. You'll see: everything's going to be different next term."

James looked doubtful, but Tamsin didn't have time to go on. If she didn't set off for Swinston very soon, she'd be late for school.

"Will you help me, James?" she said. "I want to . . . There's a sort of game I need to play. It's like blind man's buff. I have to close my eyes –" she closed them "– and you have to twiddle me round. Will you do that – please?"

James clasped her just above the knees, and twiddled. The granite chips on Ann Maria's grave crunched beneath her shuffling feet.

"Right. Now you have to close your eyes – and I keep mine closed – and I twiddle you. Have you closed them?"

James said he had. Tamsin turned him round and round.

"OK," she said. "Keep your eyes tight shut. Now neither of us knows which way we're facing. Now, I want you to count up to six – slowly."

James counted. "One. Two. Three. Four. Five. Six."

"Good," said Tamsin. "Thank you. Now we still keep our eyes shut, and twiddle each other round again."

They tried twiddling both at the same time, and ended up in a heap on top of the grave. James was gasping with laughter.

"There!" said Tamsin. "Now we can open our eyes. It's done."

They both blinked in the bright morning sunlight. Tamsin got up, shaking granite chips out of the folds of her baggy T-shirt.

"I dropped my letters," said James. "Help me look for them."

The letters were soon found, and James said to Tamsin, "Did you drop yours, too?"

"No," she said, "I threw them."

James looked puzzled.

"As you counted," she said, "I threw them, one by one, as hard as I could, in all different directions."

"You threw away *JEM1MA*?"

"I *hid* her away – so she'd be safe."

"But you'll never be able to find her again. We didn't see where the letters landed. We had our eyes shut and we don't even know which way we were facing . . . Oh Tamsin –" in his dismay, James raised a hand to his mouth and hooked the forefinger on to his lower lip "– you'll never get *JEM1MA* back!"

"No," said Tamsin. "I know."

NEW BEGINNINGS

The meeting that Tamsin's parents had proposed in their note to Mr Lively was arranged for after school on Wednesday. It had to be then because Jessie's parents weren't free on Thursday, and Friday was the last day of term. It was going to be a big meeting: Jessie's parents were going to be there – and Jessie, and everyone else who'd been invited.

It was Wednesday today, and in five minutes, school would be over. Class 1L were having their last cookery lesson with Mrs Flinch.

"I suspect," Mrs Flinch was saying, "that it's no good my asking you to do any homework this week. However, what I shall ask you to do – and to bear strongly in mind over the next six weeks –" the whole class groaned and there were protests of, "Oh, mi-iss!" "– what I *insist* that you do," Mrs Flinch went on, "is thoroughly enjoy your holidays!"

The class cheered so loudly that they had to lip-read the words, "You may go now" – and even that was difficult because, as she spoke, Mrs Flinch was doing something with her mouth that they'd never seen her do before. She was smiling.

Outside the classroom, Tamsin watched Jess and Greg go off together. She knew exactly where they were going. The meeting was to be held in the Lower School staff room, and some people would probably have arrived already.

If things had gone right, Tamsin wouldn't be here at all: she'd be miles away, wandering over the warm, sunny countryside with Jemima. But she knew by now that, given the chance, things always went as wrong as they possibly could. After all, if things hadn't gone wrong from the very beginning,

81

there'd have been no trouble and no meeting to go to now.

Well, even if she hadn't managed to run away, she still wasn't going along to that meeting. "They can't make me," she said to herself, as she walked quickly away in the opposite direction.

She walked over to the Maths and Science Block. The maths rooms were on the ground floor; biology, chemistry and physics up above. There were no children about – only a few teachers, tidying up their classrooms ready for tomorrow. Tamsin knocked on the door of Maths 5. She'd been meaning to do this for ages, but she'd never felt as desperate as she did now. What if she was too late? What if there was no one there? What if . . .

"Come in," said Miss Mayhew's voice from the other side of the door.

It was wonderful. Tamsin and Miss Mayhew sat side by side at a table, and Miss Mayhew took Tamsin's hot sticky hands into her own smooth, cool ones. There was a graph on the blackboard, which Tamsin remembered for a long time afterwards: it had a line plotted on it that went up and up until it went right up off the top of the board. The line had some surprising dips and wiggles in it, but after each one it always carried on upwards.

Miss Mayhew held Tamsin's hands clasped in hers the whole time. Tamsin explained everything, from the very beginning, and Miss Mayhew listened to it all. Whenever Tamsin's voice wobbled and petered out, Miss Mayhew started talking about the things she'd just said, and when Tamsin was ready, Miss Mayhew stopped so that she could go on again. There was never an awkward silence, never a gap where despair might have crept in.

When Tamsin came to the bit about Mrs Plummer forbidding her to go and see Jemima any more and what a disaster that had been, Miss Mayhew gave her hands a squeeze and said, "Tamsin, however much you love her, you must remember that there are lots of other good things in life – not just Jemima. You have to try to keep them all in play . . ." And Tamsin had looked up, hurt, and said, "There's nothing

82

– no one – like Jemima." And Miss Mayhew had said, "No, she does sound special. Perhaps someday you'll take me to see her, when all this has blown over?" And that had led Tamsin on to the rest of the story.

When she'd finished speaking at last, there was silence for a few moments. Then Miss Mayhew said, "Well, as for Jessie, did you know that she spends all her weekends now round at Emma Dunkley's, helping to look after Emma's pony?"

Tamsin hadn't even known that Emma Dunkley had a pony.

"No," she said, "but what's that got to do with any of this?"

"Well, caring for a pony, caring for a goat . . . What's the difference?"

"There's all the difference in the world!"

"I know, I know," said Miss Mayhew soothingly. "And *I'd* certainly prefer a goat to a pony, any day. Still, that's how I'd have put it to Jessie, if I'd been invited to go to this meeting of yours. It would have made her think about things a bit."

A short pause. Then,

"Miss Mayhew . . ." Tamsin spoke quickly, so that she wouldn't have time to stop herself. "Miss Mayhew, *will* you go? I mean, go to the meeting – instead of me?"

Miss Mayhew's eyes sparkled. She smiled the smile that had been wanting to come moments before, when she'd carefully planted the idea in Tamsin's mind. But,

"Now *there's* an idea!" she said with surprise. "And a very good one, I think, Tamsin. Yes, I really think this could be the way to put things right." She looked at her watch. "I'd better be quick, or the meeting will be over before I get there. . . . Oh, just one more thing, though." She stood up. "Could I take your diary along with me? Mr Lively has told me how vivid it is . . . In fact, I know he started getting worried some time before your mother sent him that note. Could I take it? Would you mind? It would help me a great deal in setting the record straight for everyone."

It was as if a shining angel had swooped down from the clouds and asked Tamsin if she'd mind its being her guardian. Tamsin felt suddenly that what she wanted more than anything else was sleep. She felt now that she could sleep as she hadn't slept for weeks: sleep without dreams. And, oh, she was so, so tired. She wanted to go to sleep and leave everything to her good, kind guardian angel.

"No," she murmured. "I don't mind. Yes. Please. Thank you . . . The diary's in my locker."

"Right," said Miss Mayhew, moving towards the door. "I'll pick it up on my way over. You go home. Everything will work out: you'll see."

"Yes," said Tamsin. "And, Miss Mayhew, *are* you going to marry Mr Lively?"

"Let's take one thing at a time," said the angel, and went out through the door.

Mr and Mrs Langridge didn't say much about the meeting, when they got back home on Wednesday evening, and they said nothing at all about Tamsin's not having turned up for it. What they did say was that a nice surprise had been arranged for her – a very nice surprise. Only they wouldn't tell her what it was. They said she must ask Jessie about it, because Jessie was in charge.

Tamsin arrived at school on Thursday morning determined not to say a word to Jess about anything; not to give her so much as a glance. Honestly, parents were pathetic! Thinking they could engineer a friendship with a bribe. Thinking they could trick her into talking to Jess like that. Well, they'd got another thought coming. Tamsin would show them just how much she cared for their stupid surprise. Let it crumble into dust, whatever it was! Let it rot into rags! *She* didn't want it.

Jess arrived and sat down in her place beside Tamsin. She rummaged around in her plastic sports bag, looking for her comb as usual. She found it, and started giving her hair a quick go-through before Mr Lively arrived to take registration.

Jessie's hair was long, thick and slightly frizzy. Cycle rides always blew it into a matted tangle – so, always, the first thing she did when she got to school was tidy it up as she was doing now. Whenever the comb stopped at a knot, Jess screwed her eyes tight shut, clenched her teeth and pulled.

Tamsin took no notice. At one time, she used to feel irritated that Jess didn't go to the toilets to comb her hair – and she'd hoped that the untangling of the knots really hurt. But she'd grown so used to the procedure that she couldn't even be bothered to feel irritated by it any more. She just read a book, or doodled, or finished off last night's homework, while it was going on.

Today, she was drawing a diagram of a cut-in-half buttercup, in her biology exercise book. When she'd got home from school yesterday, she'd felt too sleepy to do any homework at all, and now here was biology, this morning's first lesson, almost upon her. She must finish the diagram, because she knew that Mr Lant, the biology teacher, would be collecting in books for marking.

She'd just written 'ovum' by a tiny round blob in the middle of her buttercup, when Jess said suddenly, "D'you want a baby chick?"

Tamsin was so surprised that the only thing she could think of doing was carrying on with the diagram as if she hadn't heard. She drew an arrow pointing from the label to the blob, but she was too flustered to remember to use her ruler. She *always* used a ruler for arrows on diagrams. This arrow came out all wobbly.

What was happening? Confused, Tamsin looked up at Jess.

As soon as their eyes met, Jess closed hers and pretended to be in the middle of dragging her comb through a particularly stubborn knot. But, with her eyes tight shut and her mouth contorted into a pained grin, she said again, "Do you want a baby chick?"

Tamsin stared. "But you haven't got . . ." And then she stopped because she realized that she had no idea any more of what Jess had or hadn't got, what she did or didn't do. Jess might have sabre-toothed tigers in her bedroom and green parakeets in the loo, for all she knew. She hadn't known about the thing with Emma Dunkley's pony, had she? What was to say that Jess hadn't started keeping poultry in the back garden?

But, "I know I haven't got any," Jess snapped, finding

another imaginary tangle in her hair, and keeping her eyes screwed tight shut in more imaginary pain. "I haven't, but Pecky has." She called him Pecky – not the Pedaller. "He said, in the meeting yesterday. That's why he used to run off home straight after school: he had a hen sitting on a load of eggs, and he had to make her get off them for quarter of an hour every day, to eat and drink. They don't want to leave the nest – hens – when they're sitting on eggs, but they have to, or they starve. So Pecky got his hen off the nest every day at four o'clock."

She paused. Tamsin waited.

"And the eggs never hatched. Pecky doesn't know why. He says he did everything right, but they just never came to anything. So he began all over again, with a new lot. And this new lot was better. Day before yesterday, they hatched."

Jess was looking at Tamsin now. She sounded excited, triumphant, almost as if she'd been the one who'd so successfully kept the eggs warm the second time round.

"How many?" breathed Tamsin.

"Nine," said Jess.

"What kind?"

"Bantings."

"Bantams," Tamsin corrected.

"Anyway," said Jess quickly, "they're miniature ones. Full-grown chickens the size of mice, they'll be!"

"Bantams aren't *that* miniature," said Tamsin. "I saw pictures of them in a book I got out from the library to read about . . . ." She faltered – "a book called *Diversification for the Smallholder*. You wouldn't really notice that bantams are different from ordinary hens, unless you saw a bantam and an ordinary hen standing side by side."

"Anyway," said Jess, "Pecky said I could have some of his chicks, but Dad said I was only allowed one, and Pecky said I couldn't have one on its own because it would be lonely, and then your mum said *you* could have one and keep it round my house – like keeping a pony at livery. Pecky said that would make it OK, because then your chick and my chick could keep each other company."

Tamsin wondered what 'livery' meant. Jess saw her wanting

86

to ask, and smirked.

That made Tamsin say, "I'll keep mine at my house, thanks."

And Jess said, "You can't. People who live in council houses aren't allowed to keep livestock on the premises until they've made a special application to the Council. It takes weeks. *Years*."

"Oh," said Tamsin. And Jess stopped smirking. Perhaps she'd suddenly remembered that, if she herself was to have one of Paul's chicks, she needed Tamsin to agree to the plan. Perhaps, too, she regretted a little having been so mean.

"Oh go on, Tats," she said. "It would be great. And I thought of something else, too. If I got a girl and you got a boy – or I got a boy and you got a girl – then they could have babies of their own – and my dad wouldn't be able to stop me having more than one then. The trouble is, I asked Pecky about that, after the meeting, and he said it's impossible to tell, with chicks, which sex they are."

"No, it's not," said Tamsin. She was excited now. "Pecky's wrong. It's not impossible: just tricky. There were diagrams in *Diversification for the Smallholder* . . ."

So, after school that day, Tamsin and Jess took Tamsin's library book round to Paul's house to decide on a male and a female chick. They spent over an hour picking up peeping, scrabbling balls of yellow fluff, and comparing them to neat, black and white line drawings on a page of the book called 'Sexing Made Easy'. In the end, Paul said, "It's no good. You'll just have to take pot luck." And Tamsin and Jess didn't mind because *all* the chicks were so sweet, and felt so funny and wriggly in their hands. The only thing that they did mind was having to wait another week before Paul was willing to let the chicks go.

When Tamsin finally got home on Thursday evening, she found Mrs Plummer and James sitting in the living room with her parents. James was drinking orange juice; the three grown-ups were drinking tea.

"Ah, Tamsin," said Mrs Langridge. She didn't ask where Tamsin had been or whether she'd found out from Jess, at school, what her surprise was. She just said, "Ah, Tamsin, Mrs Plummer came round with some good news for us all – and something special to say to you."

Mrs Plummer's news was that she'd just found out she was going to have another baby. (James scowled into his glass of orange and blew bubbles, loudly, through the straw.) And the special thing for Tamsin was an apology.

Mrs Plummer sat there on the sofa, all embarrassed, saying she was sorry about the misunderstanding there'd been over Jemima. As soon as Tamsin said, "That's OK. Don't worry about it," she seemed relieved, and moved on quickly to one other thing she said she wanted to mention.

"Which is," Mrs Plummer went on, "that if you find you have any free time during the holidays, Tamsin, then any help you felt you could give me with Jemima would be most welcome. The doctor said I must try to take things a bit easy now, if I can, so it would be great if there was someone who'd be willing to bring Jemima back from the churchyard occasionally, and do the milking for me every now and then."

Tamsin started saying, "I don't think . . ." but Mrs Plummer interrupted her.

"Oh, I'm sure you'd be capable of milking on your own now. I have absolute confidence in you. And Jemima likes you so much, which is the most important thing."

"Well, that's just it." Tamsin looked miserable. "You see, she doesn't. Not any more."

"What do you mean, Tamsie?" said Mr Langridge.

But Mrs Plummer said, "Oh, I *see*." And then, "Well, if you're right, you're right – but surely you know Jemima better than to leave it at that? She's a funny old stick, but she's sensible, too. I mean, she knows what's what, doesn't she? If you give her a chance, she'll soon work out that what happened was a mistake. Give it a go, love, and you'll find that Jemima can forgive and forget with the best of them, I promise you."

Tamsin looked into Mrs Plummer's face and, for a moment, beamed. Out of the corner of her eye, she could see James strenuously mouthing something at her that looked like, "Livid dodo!" but which, she reasoned, must be, "Give it a go!"

"OK," she said.

Suddenly it seemed like years since she'd sat with Jemima at the bottom of the churchyard, with the afternoon sun warming the gravestones and the ground and Jemima's spreading sides. Suddenly she could hardly wait to feel again Jemima's shoulder leaning up against her, and watch Jemima chew and chew and flick her ears, all the time with her eyes half-closed.

"Maybe after school tomorrow," she said to Mrs Plummer. "But it won't be like before. I won't be able to come nearly as much as I used to. You see, I'm getting a chick and I've got to help my friend build a hen-house and a run."

She glanced at her parents and caught them slipping each other smiling, know-all looks. How irritating! And typical of them! Still, they couldn't help the way they behaved, she supposed. Parents were always unsubtle like that. She went into the kitchen to get herself a drink.

Friday was the hottest day they'd had that term. The hottest and the last – and, because the last, the best. Jess told Tamsin at lunchtime that she and Greg and a load of other people were going swimming in the river after school. Did Tamsin want to come along? It would be great, because Greg's big brother, Stephen, was going to climb up the old sycamore tree that leaned over the river and tie the end of a long rope high up, round one of its branches. Then they'd all take turns to swing themselves back and forth across the water – or, if they felt like it, to set off from one bank and let go of the rope half-way over, so that they dive-bombed in. Would Tamsin come? It would be brilliant fun.

It did sound fun. But Tamsin mustn't forget Jemima, waiting in Great Whenock churchyard. Still, she'd only said maybe to Mrs Plummer . . .

"Maybe," she told Jess. "I'll see." And Jess said, "OK. Right."

The last lesson of the day was Mr Lively's diary lesson – only nobody was going to do any diary-writing today.

Instead, they cleared out their lockers and tidied the bookshelves and helped Mr Lively to take down all the posters. Tamsin was grubbing up the Blu-tack left behind where 'Dickens's London' had been, when Paul walked over. He gave her a big lump of Blu-tack to use for picking off the last little traces left smeared on the wall.

"Some more eggs have hatched," he said. "Must have been last night. Four new chicks when I looked this morning."

"I didn't know you had any more to come," said Tamsin.

"Oh yes. I had two broodies, you see. I didn't show you the other one yesterday, because she was still sitting – and she's a bit nervous. I thought people crowding round might upset her."

"Oh," said Tamsin. She thought of four more little balls of yellow fluff, peeping and cheeping and scuttling away to hide under their cluck-clucking mother. "I bet they're lovely," she said.

"Yes," said Paul. "And there's a black one this time, too. Three yellow ones and a black one."

"Oh," said Tamsin again. One little black chick and all those other yellow ones! How *sweet*! Like that tea-towel design. She wondered whether Paul would want to keep the black one for himself, or whether he'd let her and Jess have it as one of their two.

"Come round and see, if you like," said Paul. "After school. She'll probably have hatched out some more by then; she had fourteen eggs under her."

Tamsin thought of Jemima in the churchyard, and she thought of Jess and the rope and the river. She wanted to laugh out loud.

"I'm not sure if I can," she said. "Can I decide later?"

"Sure," said Paul. "I'll be there anyway. Come round whenever you want."

There were twenty minutes to go to the end of school. The classroom was bare and tidy. Mr Lively called out for everyone to sit down in their places again: he had an important announcement to make, he said. Whatever it was, it seemed as if it was going to be something good, because Mr Lively

90

was grinning from ear to ear. Strangely, he'd gone very red, as well.

And then, suddenly, he was telling them that he and Miss Mayhew were going to get married.

Cheers, whistles, stamping of feet. Mr Lively was laughing and shaking his head. Then someone started *For He's a Jolly Good Fellow*! and everyone else took it up. They sang it right through to the end; then *For She's a Jolly Good Fellow*! – right through again. Mr Lively put his hands up to his face.

They had a go at *I'm getting married in the morning*, but that fizzled out because nobody really knew the words. And then Mr Lively uncovered his face (it looked redder than ever, and a bit moist round the eyes) and said, "OK, OK, that's enough. Thank you."

He went on to invite them all to a celebration party, tomorrow. He and Miss Mayhew were going to cook sausages on Swinston Recreation Ground for everyone in classes 1L and 1M.

"Oh, sir, not 1M! They stink, sir!"

"Come on, Paul," said Mr Lively. "Be a brave lad. You won't smell it in the open air."

"Gas masks provided, are they, sir, or is it bring your own?"

"Strictly bring your own, I'm afraid, Paul. But I like the idea. We'd all be grateful if you wore one, I'm sure. You can't talk with a gas mask on, you know."

The class whooped and whistled with pleasure. Paul had to shout to make himself heard:

"But sir, I haven't got a gas mask. Can I borrow yours? You must have one left over from the Second World War!"

Mr Lively was probably in his mid-twenties. The class exploded with laughter. Paul sat back in his chair and grinned.

Mr Lively was grinning too, and he was shaking his head again.

"Hope to see you all tomorrow then," he shouted above the din. "Come if you can. Gas masks or no gas masks!" And the whole class rose up and stampeded towards the door and the long summer holidays ahead.

Tamsin stood at the school gates, undecided. Paul had already gone out past her, hurrying home to his chicks. She hadn't gone with him, but that didn't mean she might not still go. "Come whenever you want," he had said. Well, she was keeping her options open. Keeping everything in play.

Now came Jess and Greg – Greg with a finger hooked round one of the handles of the bag that Jess carried slung across her back. There were five or six of the old gang with them, but among those was Tracy Darke, a new girl, whom Tamsin liked the look of, though they'd hardly ever spoken.

"You coming?" said Jess to Tamsin, as the group drew level with her. "You've *got* to come: it's too hot to do anything else except swim!" She flashed Tamsin a quick smile, and Tamsin smiled back.

The old pull. Yes, I've got to go, Tamsin thought to herself. It's the only thing to do. And then she thought of Paul and the chicks, and of Great Whenock churchyard and Jemima. No, swimming in the river *wasn't* the only thing: it would be good fun and good to have a laugh with Jess, but there *were* other things to do.

Tamsin felt Tracy Darke watching her, interested – perhaps even hopeful – and wondering what was in her mind. Well, she'll just have to go on wondering, Tamsin thought, because I don't even know myself, yet. And out loud, to Jess, she said, "You go on. I'll catch you up if I decide to come."

Greg was swinging his arm on Jess's bag, impatient of the delay. As the group moved off down the road, he said, "*Girls!*" and unhooked his finger from the bag so that he could give Jess a shove. She skipped forward, but he ran after her and put his arm round her shoulders.

Tamsin was left to her decision-making.

A car drew up, preparing to turn out through the gates and into the road. Mr Lively was in the passenger seat, Miss Mayhew driving. Tamsin pretended she hadn't seen them (although she was standing very close to the passenger door), because teachers never much liked to say hello to children outside school: it was a well-known fact. After all, if they said hello to one, then they'd have to say hello to all – or be accused of favouritism – and they could end up spending their whole lives smiling and waving to pupils they were only too glad to see the back of after school each day. Tamsin wished the car would hurry up and go.

She just glanced in at the window, and saw that Mr Lively was sitting still and staring straight ahead. Miss Mayhew was looking left and right, straining to see round the big brick gateposts, to make sure the road was clear in both directions. As Tamsin glanced down, Miss Mayhew happened to peer across Mr Lively, through his side window. Her eyes met Tamsin's – and she winked.

Then the car pulled away, gathered speed and was gone.

And Tamsin suddenly made up her mind and stepped out on to the pavement.

JEMIMA

Weeks later, in Great Whenock churchyard, Jemima was sunning herself on top of the table tomb. Her belly ballooned out comfortably on either side of her, and her legs – surprisingly slender and stick-like – were folded underneath. Sunlight reflected richly off her gleaming, chocolate-brown sides, and just caught the fine white whiskers that quivered round her muzzle as she breathed.

She wasn't expecting the girl to come, because the girl came only once in a while; but she wouldn't be surprised to see her, because, once in a while, the girl did come. It was nice when the girl came; nice when she didn't.

A thrush flew on to the tomb-top with a snail in its beak, and began cracking open the shell on the hard stone surface. *Tap – tap – tap. Tap – tap – crack.* Almost under Jemima's nose.

Jemima took no notice. The thrush ate the snail and flew off. Jemima burped – and the sound was like the gurgling of pipes in a still, quiet house. She half-closed her eyes and began to chew.

MORE WALKER PAPERBACKS
For You to Enjoy